# POOR ADVICE AND OTHER STORIES

# POOR ADVICE

LOU GAGLIA

SPRING TO MOUNTAIN PRESS

ONEONTA, NEW YORK

Spring to Mountain Press
P.O. Box 145
West Oneonta, NY 13861
springtomountainpress@gmail.com

Publisher's Note: This is a work of fiction. Names, characters, places, and incidents are a product of the author's imagination. Locales and public names are sometimes used for atmospheric purposes. Any resemblance to actual people, living or dead, or to businesses, companies, events, institutions, or locales is completely coincidental.

Cover/Art Design: Carolyn Mansir
Interior Design: www.thebookdesigner.com

Poor Advice/ Lou Gaglia. --1st ed.
ISBN: 978-0-963490-0-3

Library of Congress Control Number: 2015903842

For Marilyn, Faith, and Jim


And for my students, past and present

*Although he is a very poor fielder, he is a very poor hitter.*

Ring Lardner

*It is a bit embarrassing to have been concerned with the human problem all one's life and find at the end that one has no more to offer by way of advice than "try to be a little kinder."*

Aldous Huxley

# CONTENTS

# HANDS

I hope this letter finds you well—in fact, I hope it finds you more than well, because as you know, or maybe you can guess, I have a great fondness for you, although of course only in the form of friendship (the strictest possible form of friendship, you see) with no strings attached and with plenty of healthy platonic feeling all the way around, as they say.

Of course, people are human beings after all, and have feelings they wouldn't dare utter to anyone, let alone write down. But besides any feelings I may or may not have beyond the most platonic, strictest friendship (in every sense of the word "friendship"—or "strict"), I am writing to you (as a friend, but also as a customer of your supermarket) just to make your acquaintance in a formal way, and to ask you if you would like to meet me on Saturday for coffee, perhaps (and maybe a donut, if I may be so bold as to suggest), where we can talk about ourselves—in a strictly cashier-customer way, at first, and then perhaps eventually graduate to acquaintanceship and then to formal friendship, in the strictest handshaking-only sense, if you wish.

Besides asking you for coffee, I'd like to tell you about my past two evenings, which were funny, to say the least, but also interesting, in a way. Last night I thought I saw that man who was in the supermarket the other night, the one who yelled at you, after he wandered in and wanted to pay for a beer even though he was a dollar short. I was there, about to get on line, when he saw the manager coming and stormed away. I'd had my jar of peanut butter on me, and I held it from the lid side, just in case, but it turns out it wasn't necessary for me to step in. I remember how shaken up you looked after that, and that you rang me up with trembling hands, and that you only nodded a little when I said "bye" to you, and that you didn't even see me stop at the electric door, where I watched you for a moment as you stood wringing your hands, rubbing your left palm over your right knuckles over and over.

The incident stuck with me, I have to admit, because I saw that man last night in the street, and now tonight, after these past two evenings, with much to tell you, I've decided to be bold and invite you on Saturday for coffee at the Dunkin' Donuts at 14th Street and Union Square, at 11:00 a.m. I will be there at 10:30, well in advance of your possible arrival, so that there will be no chance of my missing you in case you're early, and I certainly hope to see you there. I will save you a proper seat, one that could not possibly give you splinters, and maybe there will be time for us to sit and talk and eat and drink and wipe our mouths with napkins. If you don't show up, I will not blame you in the least but chalk it up to a case of bad fate, and sadly, I would then have to shop at a rival supermarket— to keep my embarrassment at bay, so to speak.

This particular Dunkin' Donuts, by the way, is a nice establishment, with improved wood tables recently installed, and an excellent selection of donuts and coffee. It is right near my job at Bookmarks on 11th and Broadway. I stack and organize books, I'm sure I've told you in passing (when buying some macaroni and cheese one late afternoon, I believe). So perhaps, if you accept my invitation, we can more easily talk because I will have introduced myself already in this letter, and we can talk about you, who I am eager to hear about—as a friend, of course.

I'm sure you must guess that I have been fond of you from afar for quite some time. Or maybe you have no idea, I don't know. But in any event, I remember one afternoon a few weeks ago you asked me why I come to the supermarket every night to shop. You wanted to know, in fact, why I didn't just shop for a whole week of food in one day, why I always buy a few things here and there every night and only come over to your line, even if it's long. You were very inquisitive, very observant, I noticed, and with some amusement on my part (though I certainly wasn't laughing at you by any means) I told you that I just live from meal to meal. You laughed, I well remember, but I knew you didn't believe me because your eyebrows knit in a skewed way, which was actually very cute—platonically speaking.

"She is such a nice girl," I said aloud to myself later in the elevator on the way to my apartment, although I waited until the elevator doors closed on me, of course.


Yesterday afternoon I shopped at your market, as usual, bought my spaghetti with Ragu, thanked you for my change, and left, all too-shyly, I must say with great chagrin. I felt your hand ever so lightly touch my palm as you gave me my change, and I sighed with a little regret, longing very dearly, I admit with a blush, for a full and hearty handshake.

But all blushing to one side, I ventured out that evening to see a play on 10th Street and First Avenue. Since I have a love for all kinds of performance art, especially on TV, but also in theaters, I thought I'd take in a random play at this small independent theater and see how it was. I even pretended I was a critic on the way, stopping first to get a slice of pizza at Rose's fashionable four-table pizzeria.

The play had an odd title, *Marionettes and Donkeys*, or something like that.

"It's experimental theater," explained the ticket girl after I paid and stared with screwed-up eyes at the hand bill.

I seated myself near the back of the theater, and it filled up pretty quickly, I must say. The whole place suddenly darkened for a very long time before a spotlight in the middle of the stage lit up to a woman sitting on a barrel with no clothes on at all, so to speak. She was sad about something or other (maybe the barrel was uncomfortable), but I didn't hear anything she said. I looked at the other spectators, and they seemed so serious and wrapped up in what she was saying, but in great contrast I was wrapped up in the fact that I'd seen her around the neighborhood. She'd often had several little kids with her, and I'd seen her with them in Rose's. So as she talked to herself sadly on stage, I pictured her sitting in the pizza place with those kids—except in the same state of undress she was in at the moment—and I predicted that every time I saw her in the future I'd have to look away from her to keep from looking at her. So I got up. I found the exit, walked the long dark hallway, passed the ticket girl, and went out into civilization again, as they say.

I must tell you, that kind of theater is not my type of tea, so to speak, and it's lucky—I think now with a slight grin—that I didn't ask you to that play instead of to Dunkin' Donuts on Saturday. Not to worry, though. It is a safe bet that the workers there will be fully clothed on Saturday and there will be no chance of embarrassment, unless of course you don't come, in which case I will be embarrassed all by myself instead of both of us embarrassed in the presence of unclothed workers.

Hands

Anyway, my adventures weren't over yet, as if this wasn't
enough. I walked aimlessly around for a while, just thinking and
wishing I had my six dollars back. Then on 8th Street, I saw a crowd
gathered around a fight between two guys around my age (twenty-
eight, by the way). One of them was easily defeating the other. I
could tell because he had wrestled him to the ground and was
punching his head again and again, and the loser's head was
bloody. But as soon as he ran off, the loser got up, pulling a knife
out of his back pocket, and I recognized him as the same guy who'd
yelled at you in the supermarket. I saw the blade already opened
and I backed up along with everyone else. It made my heart jump
because at first I didn't know which way he was going to run, toward me and the others for watching, or after the guy who beat
him up. Luckily he went after the guy who beat him up, disappearing down Third Avenue. Meanwhile, I made a bee-line, as they say,
in the opposite direction, and wound up ducking into Theresa's
Coffee Shop on First Avenue.

It was late at night and crowded, so the only place to sit was on
a stool at the counter, and some young woman served me. All I
wanted was coffee, and I sat with my chin in my hand watching her
set the cup down, then pour the coffee (expertly, without spilling
any, I might add). I watched her hands slowly pour, and I frowned
deeply, I must say, because they made me think of your hands. They
were the opposite, you see. Her hands were beautiful, long and
slender and smooth, but like pictures of perfect hands a person can
see just anywhere. But your hands are slightly rounder and smaller,
and they move almost nervously when you work. I remembered
how you were wringing them after that crazy man left.

Sometimes, with just a series of glances, really, when I'm waiting
on line, I've watched your hands when they were punching numbers, or just resting quietly at your sides, and I've thought to myself,
*Well, those are her hands and no one else's hands, and that's why they're*

5

*so beautiful*. I'd recognize your hands anywhere, I'm willing to bet, even in a foreign country, years from now.

So, sitting at the counter, drinking coffee, just for the first few sips, really, I thought of your hands, because they (and you too) seemed like some great treasure that I wanted to protect, somehow. And so I was frowning (with longing, so to speak).

Now—I feel greatly disappointed to say—I couldn't possibly send this letter to you, because of the mention of your hands, which is a highly personal topic, I'm sure you'd agree. If you were to read this, you may even wish to slap my face with the very hands I just told you were beautiful. So I can't send this. Anyway, I'm willing to wager that your own manager, the guy with the mustache and beard, would probably not even pass this letter along to you, but would open it and read it himself instead, and then he and all the cashiers and the meat people would have a good laugh over it and know who I am, and I'd be the joke of the supermarket—much to my chagrin.

Bad enough that I mentioned *Marionettes and Donkeys*, and then made that awful joke about the indecent Dunkin' Donuts workers, but then I foolishly told you that the very man who yelled at you went after someone with a knife! Then of course musing about your hands was the worst of all. I'm ready to toss this letter right out the window, but then again someone might read it—or worse, mail it to you.

But I'll finish this anyway, writing the rest of it as if to you, in a manner of speaking, and streak through it and probably say more stupid things, like maybe insult your grandmother or something, which wouldn't be hard. To do, I mean...For *me* to do...

Anyway, tonight I went out again, this time to a Laurel and Hardy festival on Irving Place, not far from that Dunkin' Donuts which used to be the setting of our possible friendly meeting but now is just another overpriced donut shop.

There was supposed to be a party and then a showing of some of their films. I've always loved those two because they are extremely funny, as well as nice guys, I can tell. So I went. But when I got there, I realized that everyone else was either dressed up as Laurel, or as Hardy, and I was in my jeans and t-shirt, as usual. I stood there smiling at everyone, in a fake way, and then one of the Laurels came up to me and pretended to knock into me, the way Laurel would, and I smiled about it, but I could see that his eyes were mean, not like Laurel's eyes would have been—all innocent and nice and clumsy. This fellow's eyes weren't nice at all, so I looked away from him, but he moved closer to me anyway, like he was mad at me, and showed me his left fist which he held close to my jaw, pretending he was going to punch me. Meanwhile I stared at it, frozen, with a half-smile planted on my face. Then he punched me suddenly in the jaw with the other fist, which came out of nowhere, a light punch, just a little tap, really, but with enough force so that my head snapped back a little. Then he ran off (not the way Laurel would run) laughing and pointing at me (not the way Laurel would laugh or point either).

I wanted to leave right there, but the movies were starting, so I took a seat around all the other Laurels and Hardys. Soon I found myself cheering up because the real ones on the screen were so funny and I loved them. They were innocent, you see, and they so often got themselves hurt, but then they were always all right soon afterward. I laughed so hard at some parts that I was crying. Everyone else was laughing too, and I even forgot about that mean Laurel that punched me, except for daydreams of poking him in the eye with one finger.

I walked along St. Mark's Place on the way home. There was some game going on along the sidewalk, and people had stopped to watch. One guy kept moving around three cups with a little pea under one of them, and he called for the audience to put down twenty dollars to try their luck. A few people put down twenties, and one guy guessed right and won all the money. A woman and a man near the cup mover were the losers and they were pretty unhappy, but they congratulated the winner and threw down fresh twenties. Well, the same guy guessed right and won again. I could tell where the shell was by looking, just as well as he could, so I moved up and put a twenty down too. The man spun the cups, and when he stopped, I knew the pea was in the middle cup and turned it over, but nothing was under it. My heart jumped as he scooped up my money, and I immediately turned around and walked away, numb, feeling the crowd's eyes on me.

Walking slowly along First Avenue, I remembered those dealer's hands spinning the cups. Those other people in the audience, the winner and the losers, were in on it with him, I realized with great humiliation, and I closed my eyes for a few steps. In my mind I saw the unmoving left fist of the mean Laurel before his hidden fist bopped me.

I passed by your supermarket and peeked inside. You were behind the register. No one was on line, and you stood there almost perfectly still. I'd only glanced in for a second, but then doubled back and peered in again before heading home. That was when the idea came to me to write you this letter.

But I won't send it. My visit to the theater was supposed to be a funny story, but lasting two minutes at *Marionettes and Donkeys* wasn't funny after all. The fight was supposed to be an exciting story (without my stupidly mentioning the knife wielder's identity). The Laurel and Hardy story was supposed to be funny, too, originally, before I realized what a rotten creep that fake Laurel was. And when I first thought of telling you the shell game story, I was going to say that some other sucker lost his money.

# Hands

Worst of all, I had no idea I was going to go on and on about your hands (that just came out), or add now that when I was riding the elevator to my apartment tonight I couldn't stop remembering how they rested lonely and delicate on the register counter, so to speak, or that when I first hatched the idea of writing to you honestly and sincerely, I suddenly felt free and happy, all the way up to the nineteenth floor.

That feeling is gone now. I couldn't send this in a million years. Instead maybe I will tear it up and send something short and simple—handwritten, like one of those party invitations that kids send to other kids for birthdays, with the where and the when and the RSVP written in a column. Or better yet, come to think of it, if I really want that free and happy feeling back, maybe tomorrow afternoon I will send my own self to you. I won't say much at all, if I can help it—just breathe and say hi, spill out the where and the when, and take my RSVP like a man, as they say.

# THE LADY WITH THE RED VAN

Some guy with a televangelical smile and a red face leaned onto my gas station counter and requested a book of matches. I hesitated, having expected something more important, and slid the matches over to him.

"You know," he said, taking them up. "There's a law now against giving away free books of matches at stores."

"Oh," I said, and stared at him, wondering if he was some undercover cop, but no. He smiled like a preacher.

"But then, where would a guy ever get matches," he asked, tilting his head, "if they're not for free anymore?"

"Maybe the supermarket," I said. "Or maybe a guy could just look on the internet and do a search on where to buy matches."

He chuckled. "Or maybe a guy could do a search on how to get matches for free anyway." He squinted one eye at me and nodded his head like he'd made a point, and I faked a smile. He was about to say something else but the bell on top of the door rang, and a middle-aged lady stuck only her head inside.

"You know, you didn't have to come in here and take your sweet time!"

I thought it was the televangelist's wife because he heaved a big sigh, stuck out his jaw, and showed his bottom teeth.

"Lady, there are eleven pumps out there, all empty."

She came all the way inside and stood near the door. "You could have pulled up, you know. You left me no room."

"Holy crap, lady," said the preacher, giving her a wild look. "Eleven empty pumps."

"That's not the point."

"It *is* the point."

"You could still move up," she said, and stormed out.

The preacher stared at me wide-eyed. "You know, maybe I'll use these matches on her. Maybe I will."

As he strode away, I casually suggested that lighting up ladies at gas stations wasn't safe. He smiled back at me as he swung open the door and headed for pumps eleven and twelve where I watched him smirk at her and look her up and down while she waited, arms folded, for him to pump his gas.

He didn't grace the gas station with his presence again, at least not while I patrolled the register, but the middle-aged lady with the enormous hairdo continued to show up. I recognized her red van in the left turn lane a few times, and each time, sometimes twice in one day, she hurried to her spot at pump eleven, and didn't even move up naturally to pump twelve when the coast was clear ahead of her. It was pump eleven all the way or bust.

Once, when someone beat her to pump eleven, she tore around the car and screeched to a stop long enough to glare at a big guy who was easing himself out on the driver's side, with no idea he was being threatened by her knit eyebrows. I laughed, and so it became part of my 9 a.m. routine to watch her furious race to pump eleven.

One morning the match issue resurfaced when a skinny guy with yellow teeth and an unshaved face asked me for a book.

"What book?" I asked.

"Book-a-matches. Waddaya think?" he said.

"Oh. Matches...well, they're not free no more," I said. "They have boxes of them in the aisle there."

"What do you mean they ain't free? I been coming here for years (I'd never seen the guy), pal."

"Well, there's a new law—"

"I don't care about any damn new law. This is America, isn't it? I want a book of matches, toot sweet."

His face was all red, and so I drifted to where my ping pong paddle rested under the counter. When a guy that scraggly says "toot sweet" to you, you get your back up and your heart races a little.

"I want an answer, punk," he went on.

The word "punk" made my belly shiver with adrenaline. "Bunk" or "junk" wouldn't have had any effect on me in the least, and "thunk" would have made me look around for what fell, but at the word "punk" I examined his forehead for a soft place to whack with my paddle if he got too close.

Over his shoulder I saw that the lady's red van had pulled up to pump eleven, except that some pick-up truck was in front of her at twelve, so that she had to angle her van to get the hose to reach. I shrugged to the unshaved face.

"I can maybe give you a light if you want."

"I don't want a damn light, one damn light. I want a book of matches, for free. Told you that. I told you already what I wanted."

Then a guy with a bushy white beard and wearing khakis, who'd been sitting at the lone table near the window having coffee, spoke up.

"Hey, it ain't his fault. It's the fault of the companies that sell lighters and are in bed with the whole state. They have conspired to manipulate the fire industry for their own profits and won't allow a struck match without it costing us taxpayers our hard-earned money which we have made off the sweat of our brows." This guy was talking slow and calm, and his voice was deep and gravelly, and his wispy beard made little jutting waves as he talked. The match nut frowned impatiently, and he glanced over like he wanted to get back to threatening me, but the guy in khakis went on after taking a short sip of coffee.

"It is our sworn resolve, then, to be kind and neighborly to each other, not always blindly obey the higher-ups in the upper echelons of society who want to control us and our matches. So, my friend, even though it cramps up your style to purchase some needed matches at a discount store, it is not the fault of this here fellow who is just scraping by at a gas station job. And you, my friend," he went on to me, "even though it is against the law, it wouldn't be any skin off your considerable nose to give this here fellow a simple and free book of matches just this one time out of the kindness of your heart, for him to take and share with the bosoms of his family in his own home sweet home."

He stopped to sip at his coffee, and I fingered the paddle and looked for a soft spot on his forehead too. Then in walked that lady, the bell over the door ringing furiously behind her. Her minivan was still at pump eleven, parked all crooked.

"Is that someone's truck out there?" she asked all three of us.

"It is the truck of yours truly," said the guy in khakis.

"You know, you didn't have to park so that I can't pump my own gas."

"Well, that is neither hither nor thither, Ma'am," began the man, taking another sip.

"Oh, don't thither me. You are sitting here in cold blood having coffee while parked at a pump where honest people are trying to get their gas."

"Lady, it would behoove you to understand that a man can park wherever he likes at this station because there are twelve pumps out there and no cars hardly never come in. Why don't you take your keys and get in your car and drive around to one of those empty pumps?"

The man who wanted free matches had been looking down at his feet, but he growled and stomped away like he couldn't take anymore.

"You have interrupted my morning coffee in front of my favorite window, Ma'am," continued the man with his wispy beard, "and you are worrying me over a gas pump, while in other countries—Hawaii, for instance—children are starving, and in some cities like California there is rioting in the streets and dogs roam around naked. It don't take no genius to figure out that there are far more important matters than your difficulties with the parked position of my truck. So it behooves me to tell you—"

"Could you just move your car up," the woman said, biting at her full row of nails.

"I would be honored to take your request into consideration, Madame, but first—"

"Because you're really making me nervous—"

"First...like I'm trying to tell you, I will have to finish my coffee here and maybe have a crumb cake or two."

"Could you please stop talking and move that truck?"

I sat down on a red stool, away from the cash register, and watched her bite down on her nails.

"Well..." began the man in khakis, but she turned and burst out the door the same way the unshaved face had. Then she waited in front of her car for a while before getting into the driver's seat and gripping the wheel. The man in khakis continued to sip his coffee and then bought a crumb cake, and the lady sat there for another half hour while the man ate and drank a refilled cup. Some customers came in, and one of them asked for matches but only sighed when I told him about the new state law. Finally, the man in khakis left, but he edged his truck forward only little by little while she moved up too, herky and jerky—letting out a murderous scream at one point—until I almost couldn't take it anymore myself and started outside. At last, though, he drove away at normal speed and exited into traffic, and she hurried to pull up and straighten out so she could back up properly to her pump, but someone in a Corvette beat her there. She screamed out the window like a horror movie extra to a young woman sitting behind the Corvette's wheel, and then she pealed out of the station.

The next morning the man in khakis was back, his truck parked at pump five this time. He sipped at his coffee and ate crumb cake and said nothing, and at nine o'clock the red van pulled alongside pump eleven. She hurried to pump gas and left, but she'd only been there a minute or two so I walked outside to check the pump. Two dollars showed. When I got back inside, I thought for a long time about asking the man in khakis what he thought, but I stayed quiet while he looked out the window and seemed to laugh.

At around 8:30 the next morning, I grabbed two orange cones from the back and placed them in front of pump eleven. The man in khakis, parked at pump two, had just poured coffee when I returned. He sighed and sat down and sipped, and I waited. After 9:00 I saw her red van pull into the left lane and slow down hesitantly before turning into the station. The van idled in front of the first cone, and she sat with her forehead on the steering wheel for a good five minutes.

"She ain't leaving," coughed the man in khakis. "She'll stay there all day because she has a mission in life and this is it."

"How do you know?" I asked him.

"People are starving in Canada, you know, and this woman has made pumping a little gas her life's goal. It's a little like that guy the other day who wanted to kill you because of the matches you withheld from him."

"Kill me? No, he was just mad."

16

"He was mad that you had put a crimp in his life, for no apparent reason except for some random law, but he was prevented from taking your life away because I was sitting here whilst he went off the deepest of ends."

"Well, maybe he would have killed you too, then."

"I am hard to kill, my friend, so that is highly doubtful, because I have a large belly and big old beefy arms, and so it would be hard to stab me through and through, but that guy would have drove a knife into you easy—like butter on popcorn and no problem—and then just strolled on out, if not for me sitting here and taking up precious space at this lonely table."

I pointed a rigid finger at him. "You need to leave."

"So the next time a guy asks you for matches, just give him his precious accoutrements, so that you can make it home in one piece into the bosoms of your loved ones."

"I'm calling my boss. You need to go," I said, and hurried outside. The lady in the van at pump eleven was resting her cheek on the steering wheel, her arms at her sides.

"Lady," I said, "this was out of service, but it's okay now. Pull right up." I took the cones away and watched her trembling hands on the wheel as she pulled up, and then I stood nearby while she tried to slide her shaky credit card into the pump's slot. "It's all right," I found myself saying to her two or three times.

"There's all kinds of people in the world," philosophized the man as soon as I stepped back inside, and I rolled my eyes and frowned my way behind the counter. "Everyone's a nut about something or other." He sipped his coffee. "A lot of people in the Andes Mountains, for instance, don't even know which end is up."

"What people? What the hell are you talking about?" I sputtered, and spotted the woman making her way toward the door.

"I'm talking about people everywhere: executives in banks, for instance...shed architects, erosion surveyors, corn syrup tasters, scarecrow stuffers, sword swallowers—as well as other people from all walks of life," he concluded, and I pinched at the space between my eyes.

The bell rang above the door and the woman entered.

"Could you put those cones down at my pump again tomorrow, about nine o'clock?" she asked me from the door, and I nodded to her with a horrified glance. She swung open the door and walked out, but then poked her head back in. "But could you move them up a little? Maybe about six inches, okay? Then my hose could be perfectly in line...and my spout could go straight into that, you know, hole in the tank."

# A LOST FLOKATI

## The Seagulls

This morning began the third day of my self-improvement mission, which so far I give mixed reviews. It includes nightmares that I have brought on myself, and breakfasts at the diner near the harbor where I make sure to eat good food—like only a few strips of bacon and not so much butter on my toast, all of which I chew twenty-four or more times per bite. This last new habit almost made me late for work, but so did watching two seagulls fight over a fish on the dock before I reached my car. One seagull had caught a big fish, which he tried to swallow in a hurry because another seagull was pestering him. The one with the fish flew far enough away to drop it, but the other one closed in, keeping the pressure on and causing the beleaguered gull to try swallowing it whole. I was afraid he was going to choke himself to death. Finally, though, the chased gull dropped his breakfast on the dock a second too long and the pesky one clamped onto it and flew away. That was pretty smart of him; meanwhile, the not-so-smart seagull hopped around looking dazed. If I was him, I'd have been pecking at myself for not thinking of flying far away with the fish to a nice secluded spot to eat in peace and quietude.

This self-improvement plan of mine includes paying more attention (like to seagulls), listening to people more, reading more, remembering my dreams more, and refraining from losing my temper because it can be pretty bad, especially last summer when I played baseball in the Connie Mack League. But now, at twenty, I am already too old for Connie Mack, and it is time to get serious and improve all facets of my life because my job is the same one I had in high school. And I'm not even married yet. And I still live with my grandmother.

There is a dream book on my bedside table that I am determined to write in every morning when I wake up. I heard somewhere that a person can control his own dreams if he says aloud, "Tonight I will control my dreams." I tried it the last two nights, but both times I wound up having uncontrollable nightmares instead. Two nights ago, for instance, I dreamed about my grandmother. She was just sitting there reading or something—it was a nothing dream—but when I figured out it was only a dream she got a wild look to her. I tried to open my eyes to real life, but the dream wouldn't end, and my own sweet grandma stood up to come after me—quick, not like my real grandma. I finally forced myself awake just before she got to me.

Then last night I had a dream about lying around at the beach with a pretty girl, but as soon as I thought, this can't be real, she disappeared, only to be replaced by a bunch of guys in turtlenecks stretching piano wire at me. I tried to open my eyes wide—again, again—before waking up for sure. My heart hammered and I turned over and cursed at myself for interrupting a girl-on-the-beach dream in the first place.

I was preoccupied with seagulls and dreams when I walked into work at the rug cleaning plant, and right away Harry, an old guy with a full beard who either grouches at me or jokes around with me, muttered a complaint from behind his desk.

"You lost Mrs. Thompson's flokati," he said, looking down at the works of the calculator he'd been trying to fix yesterday.

"I didn't lose it. I know I put it in bin nine. I know it for a fact."

"It's not in bin nine," Harry mumbled. "Get those orders you took yesterday, the three steam jobs. No pick-ups today."

"Good, cause my back—"

"Damn you, calculator." He gave it a shake, then looked up. "Punch in, will you, I want to be alone with this thing." I went into the back room and punched in. "But look for that flokati before you go. Who the hell knows where it is..."

I went into the bin room and straight to bin nine, which was empty. "Where's the flokati?" I called.

"That's what I'm telling you. It's not in bin nine. Maybe it flew back to Greece."

I came back into the front room, confused. "I put it there..."

"Get on the road, will you? I gotta fix this thing."

## Northport

Across the street from the docks and the band shell is Fairview Road, which is high up and lined with houses for the very rich. That's where my first stop was, right near where I'd seen those seagulls fighting an hour before. I hadn't thought anything of the name typed on the first invoice until the door opened to Jamie Morrow, standing at the entrance in a bikini. I hadn't seen her since our junior year in high school, when it took me almost the whole year of practicing in front of mirrors to ask her out in May, between classes. I had to chase her down the hallway while she listed all the reasons why she was so busy—and "thanks anyway," she sang.

I hated her after that one-minute race through the history wing and all over again after she opened the door—so beautiful there that I wouldn't even glance at her—and led me into her hallway. I looked everywhere but at her, trying to fool myself by pretending that maybe she was just some crabby old lady from Speonk.

The rug on the stairs needed to be steam cleaned, she said, plus the first three upstairs bedrooms, as well as the downstairs hallway where we stood. I nodded like I was listening, but all of what she said was on the invoice anyway. I set my face like stone, imagining the present twenty-year-old smarter me beating the hell out of the seventeen-year-old idiot me for running (slap) after (slap) the impossible (bonk). I held out the invoice for her to sign, looking up the stairs at the job ahead. Then she told me—her voice soft, a sneak attack—that the check was on the table in the foyer and she'd be out back if I needed her.

I wasn't going to need her or chat with her or even nod her way, I vowed, heaving the steam machine up the stairs and starting on the first room. Big beautiful house. And me from the poor side of town, on the wrong side of the tracks, like poor George Wilson from *The Great Gatsby,* whose own wife said he wasn't fit to lick her shoe. Just when I was thinking that maybe Wilson would have liked that, I pulled back too hard on the hose handle and my elbow knocked a statue off a desk. The statue, some jockey/horse combination, hit only carpet, but it broke cleanly in two anyway. I stopped everything and picked up the two pieces–plus another tiny chipped piece that I stuck in my pocket–and fit them together again. It took me a couple of minutes to get it to stand up without tipping over, and then I looked at it for a minute, confused. The jockey on the horse had broken mid-waist, and the top half of his body was just as big as his bottom half plus the whole horse combined. Carefully steam-cleaning and backing my way out of the room, I missed spots on purpose, just spraying them wet instead.

The other two rooms and the stairs were uneventful, but it was getting hot. Jamie hadn't offered me a drink, and from the downstairs hallway, dripping sweat from my chin, I saw the reason: she was out in the courtyard, "busy" lying on a beach chair getting a tan. That was playing with fire, letting the sun cook her like that, as far as I was concerned, and I just snuck out because she'd already signed the invoice.

## Nissequogue

That whole episode at Jamie Morrow's really put me in a mood, so I had early lunch at the pizza place on Main Street before heading over to a town called Nissequogue, which I had trouble finding. The lady there, in her thirties, maybe, had two little kids she kept in a pen in the dining room. When I said hi to them and smiled, the lady looked mad.

I had to steam the living room rug and the kids' room rug, which both looked like they'd been drooled on. I was halfway through the living room before realizing that I was running out of steam cleaning solution, so I had to call Harry to bring more.

"Where the hell are you?" he asked me over the phone. I looked across the kitchen table at the woman, who looked even madder than before.

"Uh...in uh..." I looked at the invoice. "I'm in Niss-socki."

"Niss-a-kwog!" the woman fumed at me.

"Uh...Niss-a-kwog, Harry," I said into the phone, and looked at the woman blankly because she was really steamed.

A half hour later Harry brought me a gallon of cleaner, but he didn't look as mad as I thought he would. He just said something about needing to get back to his calculator.

The woman was the mad one; still, later while I was cleaning the kids' room, she brought me something to drink, and I thanked her very much. She was all right, this lady, to give me a soda even though I'd mispronounced her town. I flipped the top open but stopped myself before sipping. It was diet soda. Diet. Filled with saccharine. What was with people, I wondered, drinking saccharine and baking in the sun, set on killing themselves. I didn't want to take the chance, so after calculating the result of every possible action, including her angry one if I said I didn't want the drink after all, I poured the saccharine soda into the steam machine. It wasn't so much compared to all the water sloshing in it, I reasoned while finishing the kids' room.

## Bay Shore

Finally, at around three o'clock I arrived at house number three. No girl in a bikini, no angry-eyed mother of penned-up tots in a dining room, just an old lady who greeted me like I was her grandson. She had a house filled with books, including shelves of them in her kitchen. She didn't get around to telling me where to work until she'd shown me a bunch of old books in her living room. I told her I liked to read.

"I love European literature," she said. "Especially the Russians. Here's my Tolstoy collection."

"Wow. I read his story about a horse."

"*Kohlstomer*. Beautiful story." She pulled out a book and leafed toward the back. "Here it is."

I looked toward the upstairs where I figured the rugs were.

"Read...right here," she said, outlining a passage with her forefinger. "Read this."

"All right." I began to read.

"Out loud." I looked up. "Read it out. I love to hear it."

"...Okay." I read:

*But I will not speak of that unfortunate period of my first love; she herself remembers my mad passion, which ended for me in the most important change of my life.*

24

*The strappers rushed to drive her away and to beat me. That evening I was shut up in a special stall where I neighed all night as if foreseeing what was to happen next.*

"Beautiful passage," she said when I finished.

"Sounds scary."

"The way he can catch experience, even of a horse..." She drifted off into the kitchen.

"Well," I said to the kitchen wall, "it beats *Black Beauty,* that's for sure."

I picked up my machine and the cleaning fluid and was looking around for a dirty carpet when she came out with a book. "Here are some more of Tolstoy's stories. Try 'Master and Man.' What an incredible story."

"I can't bring it back, though."

"Well, I've got an Oriental rug in the den I want you to clean. You can bring it back next week."

"Oh." I thought of my lower back. "All right."

I rested the book against the door where I wouldn't forget it and finally got myself upstairs to work on two large bedrooms. I didn't break any statues or spill artificial sweetener into the machine's tank or miss any spots. I liked this lady, and tried to make it my best job of a long day that had begun with that poor harried seagull losing its fish and ended with a warm thank you from an old woman who'd lent me a book and asked me to read Tolstoy to her.

## Calculations

The flokati was in bin eight the whole time. I called this out to Harry from the bin room, and he took a long time before answering. "What are you, dyslexic or something? Come here and help me figure out this damn calculator, because I have no idea."

I went into his office after punching out. "I don't get how I didn't see the flokati right next—"

"Oh. Morrow called. She said to come back for your tip."

"My tip?"

"Yeah." He sat back in his chair, rubbing his eyes. "And Magiliagutti or Magliagory or whatever her name is from Bay Shore, she called."

"Really?" I thought about the book, which I'd left in the van.

"She complained that you took too long."

I stood there next to his desk, eyebrows furrowed.

"I don't know what to do with you," he said, shaking his head down at the calculator. "Putting a flokati in the wrong bin. Not finding it when it's staring you right in the face." He peeked at me over his glasses and smirked. "Reading books to old ladies."

I opened my mouth to say something but he waved his hand with a chuckle.

"Just come here and help me figure this damn thing out."

On the way home, I adjusted my self-improvement plan slightly, starting with dreams. I've decided to leave myself alone in them, whatever happens, so I don't ruin a good thing. And may the beach girl appear in at least one dream. And may my grandma not show up in it.

# POOR ADVICE

My old friend Rich had a stroke about a year ago, but this story isn't about him. I just bring him up because he's 300 pounds and likes to give me advice on exercise. Move your arms around, he says, and stretch and touch your knees. Sway from side to side, he says. Funny, and I thought playing eighteen holes of golf was good exercise. And about eating he might say, I didn't eat that much today, just a couple of hot dogs and a pizza. Or, I'm cutting down on my sodium. But what about the hot dogs? I'd say. Oh, he'd retort, I don't eat hot dogs that much, and I cut down on the pot pies, too.

He'll talk about the Mets forever, and whom they might trade a year from now, but if there's anything serious to be discussed he finds a way to change the subject. Like this woman I'm interested in. She works down on Elizabeth Street at the Chinese bakery and has the prettiest eyes and smile I've ever seen. Well, it seemed she was interested in me, too, and we would start talking when I came in for my afternoon iced coffee. But then, as usual, I had a tough time asking her out. Since I'm pushing thirty-five, twenty-years gone are the days when one of my buddies might check the girl out for me, or say to her, Hey, do you like him? He sure likes you. And since I'm not exactly a guy who spills his guts to every friend I have,

I still sometimes wind up calling on my old childhood pal Rich for advice.

So one day I tried to talk to him on the phone about the bakery woman, just in passing, but after I deflected the conversation about the Mets' weaknesses and steered it back to her, all he would say was, Just take it slow. Take it easy. Relax. No sense in worrying about it.

Take it slow. I'm almost forty and unmarried and super-shy and chickening out on another chance all over again. He knew as much about women as about exercise. So after thinking for a few days, I decided to force myself into asking her out. I went right out and bought two tickets to the opera. Orchestra seats. Saturday matinee. *La Boheme.* And wouldn't she love to go, cooped up for seven days, ten to twelve hours a day in that bakery? I hoped so. I stuck the tickets in my pocket, which meant I'd either have to ask her to it or eat one of the tickets. Great plan, huh?

A day or two after I bought the tickets I paced up and down Elizabeth Street for a while before I went in there for iced coffee. She looked right at me, and I waved and smiled to her, but she just looked away like she didn't know me. The smile stayed frozen on me while some lady with big teeth came at me for my order. I guessed she was busy or something, but it was the first time I didn't get the beautiful smile and hello.

I went in there again the next day. She looked right at me when I walked in. I smiled to her but she looked away again. No wave. No hello. What the—

The opera was a week away. I paced Elizabeth Street and went to three rival bakeries and had four iced coffees in me before I stepped into her bakery. She looked right at me when I came in, and this time smiled and said, Iced coffee? I hadn't expected the smile, and I'd already turned to the teeth lady. Iced coffee, I growled. Expecting to be snubbed again, I had done the snubbing this time.

Well, the snubbing score was 2-1 with her in the lead, but I don't think it made a difference to her because the next day when I went in with a smile on my face, she just glanced at me dourly and drifted away. The next morning, she looked right at me when I went in, and I smiled and said a cheerful hi, but she almost shouted, "Yes?" and then proceeded to get very busy with other customers while I ordered hot coffee through another girl.

The opera was only a few days away, and all seemed lost. I went in one more time, but we only looked at each other blankly. She got very busy again, and after a few moments, without ordering, I slipped out.

Meanwhile, the two tickets to *La Boheme* were still stuck in my pocket, bent from being carried to the bakery every day to show her. I wasn't going to ask anyone else because my heart was set on her, so I decided to go alone.

I sat there in the orchestra seat next to her empty one and realized pretty quickly that it was going to be no fun pretending she was there. I wasn't in the mood. I put *The Daily News* on the seat as her replacement.

The opera was only a little familiar to me. I had the libretto and decided to keep myself busy trying to figure out what was going on in the story. The libretto was all in Italian, so it wasn't much help. I had visited Italy alone fifteen years before and could only be understood by the natives when I spoke English. The only Italian word I knew was "basta!" which is what my grandmother used to say to me and my cousins when we were laughing too much. For my entire childhood and adolescence I'd thought she was calling us bastards. Anyway, without knowing the words, this is what I gathered from the opera.

When the curtain opened there was some poor guy trying to write, but he kept getting up, maybe because there was a draft or he thought there was a mouse. Then some big guy with a deep voice busted in and they sang for a while about the draft or the mouse. Pretty soon the big guy said he had an AA meeting so he split, and then this lady with her teensy voice "accidentally" walked in, and she said something like she was looking for a nudist camp and must have come to the wrong place. Well, this got the writer all worked up and he said to wait and talk a while, and pretty soon they were getting along all right, although she kept singing with her back to him and fluttering all around the room like some bird—maybe to keep him from getting bored or so he might lose some of the extra poundage. In any case, she had him prancing all around the room and wrapped around her little finger.

After a little while, she threw her ring on the floor and pretended like she had lost it. The two lovers got on hands and knees to search it out, and while they were groping around for it, their hands touched together. I don't even know if they found the ring, but when they got to their feet, still holding hands, the music got all swollen. He started booming out with a big old song about her dishpan hands, and I have to admit that a little teardrop was curling down my right cheek as I thought about singing like that to the bakery woman with the other workers looking on and the customers waiting around impatiently, my voice booming all the way down Elizabeth Street and she smiling right into my face.

When the song ended I clapped along with everyone else as the two lovers stood on stage like statues waiting for everyone to shut up, and then the girl started in on the next song, tweeting that her name was Mimi. Her beautiful voice went through me like a nail, and the way it sounded she was singing her entire life history to him while he stood there all wrapped up in her looks but pretending to listen.

When her song was all done, there was an even bigger uproar from the crowd, but this time I didn't do any clapping. I disliked her automatically because she was almost as pretty as the bakery woman, even way up on stage, and I was jealous of the writer who seemed to have all the luck. I couldn't even get an iced coffee, much less a smile or a wave or her name from her, and here was this guy lucking into a girl just because he could write and sing a little and had a full complement of hair.

I missed a little of the story because I was daydreaming, but soon there was another happy couple hanging out with Mimi and Rudolpho and having a great time. They sat in a café discussing proper horse care while cardboard appeared from the heavens pretending to be the street. Pretty soon Mimi had trouble keeping down the crepe suzette, and everyone looked at her, but it was a false alarm and they ordered a pitcher of beer and discussed somnambulism. All was well until one of the cows started mooing too loud and an extra had to lead him backstage to be slaughtered. Mimi began hacking again because she was allergic to the other girl's perfume, and Rudolpho finally decided to take her home before she ruined all their fun.

At halftime everyone went to the bathroom but I stayed in my seat, glancing through the program and wondering vaguely whether it was that the bakery woman had suddenly noticed I was losing my hair and that was why she'd stopped smiling. By the time the second act started I hated her, and I didn't even follow the story that much but slipped in and out of sleep. I finally woke up for good when Mimi went into one of her most vicious coughing jags, hacking up a storm while everyone except the horses looked on worried. Before she knew it she was in bed dying, and the writer was bent over her, not even minding that she was coughing right in his face—a sure sign of true love when a girl can cough in a guy's face and he doesn't even flinch or get pissed.

At last she croaked permanently and the writer went ape and bawled his head off, singing all the while, but I wasn't too sad at that part and was thinking, big deal if she's dead, because at least he had the chance to have a girl love him and die on him. I was sadder at the beginning when they touched hands, and that should have been the end of the whole opera right there, with everyone going home to use their own bathrooms.

When it ended there was a big hubbub over the actors coming back on stage for a final farewell, with the biggest bravos of all saved for Mimi when she came out healthy again. I stopped clapping at her grand entrance, but then clapped again for one of the horses when he stuck his head through a scenery window looking for some respect.

I walked all the way home from Lincoln Center because I didn't want to be around anyone, not even the typically friendly New York cab driver. An hour later when I reached Elizabeth Street, I passed the bakery. It seemed about to close. Casually, I peeked inside and spotted her walking with a broom in front of the cake cases. Seeing me, she stopped dead for a second, and I gave her a little wave. She hesitated, looked full at me, and then waved back—the wave as small as mine but the smile just as warm. Then she hurriedly disappeared behind the counter.

With Rudolpho still singing in my head, I went in for an iced coffee before she closed.

# DAYS OF WINE AND PRATFALLS

Jack's nightly dinners at the pizza restaurant after work were routine until the new waitress handed him a hot plate of baked ziti.

"Yow!" Jack cried, shaking both hands wildly and then plunging them into the pitcher of ice water.

The waitress giggled, and he looked up at her curiously.

"I'm really sorry." She put her hand to her mouth and continued to chuckle. "Are you all right?"

"No, it's my fault," he said, taking his hands out of the pitcher.

"It was hot," she said.

"Thanks. I know."

While he ate, he read his newspaper, as usual, but sneaked looks over at the waitress as she cleaned a table with a rag. He watched her accidentally wipe the entire oil and vinegar stand onto a booth seat, then laugh to herself as she picked it up, wiping the spilled liquid off with her hand.

Jack looked away out the window, into the dark street. His eyes opened wider. "Jeez," he said to himself aloud, "I think I'm in love."

Her name was Lee, and she thought he looked pretty cute in his oil delivery man's uniform. She felt bad that she'd burned his fingers, especially since he didn't get angry, didn't ask for a new pitcher of water, and left her a nice tip. A few nights later, as she walked by his table, she got one foot stuck under another and fell against his table, then rolled backwards into him. He caught her, helped her to her feet, and asked her to a movie.

On the way into the movie theater she accidentally swung the glass door into his nose. "Sorry," she said, wincing, but he laughed it off.

As they made their way into the middle of an aisle she caught her coat on one of the seats, and as they both bent to untangle it, they knocked heads.

I'm crazy about her, Jack thought as they finally settled into their seats and held hands. Head over heels. She's so beautiful in her clumsiness.

Later he bought an extra-large tub of popcorn and held it lightly between them on the arms of their seats. But when he relaxed his grip a little, she sneezed violently, knocking the entire contents into his lap.

Lee's relationships had never lasted more than a few dates. The last man in her life was her boss in an insurance office where she was secretary. She'd told him she fixed the squeak in his chair, but when he sat in it, it tipped completely backward and over. She'd forgotten that she'd released that thingy, the whatchamacallit underneath the chair to wipe it clean, and had forgotten to snap it closed again.

Lee felt that it was only a matter of time before Jack stopped calling her. But his burned hands hadn't bothered him, the door into his nose was no big deal, and he'd eaten the buttery popcorn right off his lap without a complaint. Maybe it would work out after all, but she wasn't counting on it.

◇◇◇

When they began living together at his house, he loved her so much that the accidents hardly ever bothered him. One Saturday, while they tried to get the hose to work, she turned the water on at the wrong time, catching him full in the face with a steady blast. Weekends later they were painting the house together. He took the hallway and she took the bathroom, but just as he decided to take care of the outside door frame of the bathroom, she turned the corner at the same time and painted his face with a neat stroke.

Lee's boss at work became increasingly frustrated with her. It wasn't only the burning of customers' hands with baked ziti dishes and pans of pizza. It was the tripping into diners, the annoying questions she asked the pizza makers just as they were tossing their pies, only to have the pies land on the floor or their heads. It was turning on the coffee machine but forgetting to put the pot underneath. It was her uncanny ability to conk heads with the cooks and waiters and the boss himself no matter how careful they'd become around her. Finally, she accidentally poured ice water down a woman's back, missing the glass entirely. Her boss had had enough and finally dismissed her.

Jack was never especially clumsy himself. But one morning, as they brushed their teeth side by side, he dropped his toothbrush. "I've never done that before," he remarked, but she was still too sleepy to notice or answer. A few days later, in the garage, as they headed for one of the cars on the way to the supermarket, he dropped one apple under one car and another apple under the other. They were too far under to reach, so he backed one car out and ran the apple over; then he backed the other car out, more carefully, but ran that one over, too.

"You're getting to be worse than me," she noted, chuckling over the two smashed apples.

"That's impossible," he laughed.

Lee found another job, this time as a museum cashier. She worked her first three days without an accident. On the fourth day, as she was handing a man his change, she slipped and fell with a thump and the change flew into the air. But she went the entire following week without a pratfall, a spill, or even a head bonk. Even her trips to the cafeteria for lunch were almost incident-free.

During a break she looked idly at some museum brochures listing the goings-on around town, and noticed that the gym offered Yoga classes. She thought she'd give it a try.

Jack and Lee tried to clear space in the backyard for a garden. As they walked single file along the grass near scattered garden tools, Lee stepped to the side. "Watch the— (behind her, Jack stepped on the forked end of a rake and the handle walloped him in the forehead) —rake!" she finished as he staggered. He groaned, then laughed, feeling at the bump on his forehead, but she looked at him gravely. "Are you all right?" she asked, and ran inside for ice.

At work Jack was in the middle of his route, filling a house's oil tank. When a hummingbird scared him he ran back to his truck, but he was clipped by a kid on a bicycle as he crossed the sidewalk. By the time he got up and brushed himself off, he realized he'd overfilled the tank. Oil spilled all along the walkway on the side of the house when he released the hose. He tried to clean the spill with extra rags he had in the truck, but it didn't help much, so he broke large branches off a neighbor's bushes and placed them over the spill. It was lucky, he thought, that neither the neighbor nor the house's owners were home. Maybe they wouldn't notice the spill or the missing branches.

◇◇◇

Lee's Yoga lessons were fascinating and relaxing to her. She found she could center herself and balance. "I can stand on one leg for hours," she boasted to a friend over the phone.

"Why would you even want to balance on one leg for hours?" her friend had answered.

Her friend didn't understand. No one did.

"Who balances for hours on one leg?" the friend went on. "I never heard of such a thing."

"I'm swimming, too," Lee interrupted. "I can swim all day. Before, whenever I swam, I'd just sink. Now I can float all—"

"I gotta get off the phone," her friend cut in.

In the kitchen at home, Jack decided to put up a photo of him and Lee at the beach. Lee sat at the table reading a Yoga book while Jack found the stud and expertly began to drive a nail through. But as he hammered the nail one final emphatic time, the frying pan fell off the shelf above and dinged Jack on the head. The noise made Lee look up from her book. As Jack staggered around holding his head and laughing, Lee spat out, "Why in the world are you hanging that picture in the kitchen?" He stopped staggering to stare at her annoyed face. She went angrily back to her book, and he slumped sourly into a kitchen chair.

Lee found herself avoiding marbles scattered in the hallway leading to the kitchen. She caught a bag of rice before it came down on her as she opened a cabinet. She knew she hadn't put the rice up there or placed the marbles in the hallway. A few days later she walked into the kitchen and was caught by surprise by the wet floor. She gripped the floor with her bare feet to keep from slipping before expertly cat-walking away.

Jack was miserable. The marbles, the rice, the wet kitchen floor—none of it had worked. He was losing her.

After he finished his deliveries, he'd sometimes go out to eat dinner alone rather than eat at home. He went to the same pizza restaurant where he'd met Lee. The waitress cheerfully warned him well ahead of time about the hot dish of baked ziti. He didn't even leave her a tip.

The museum director asked Lee out to lunch at a fancy French restaurant. She was thrilled, but she felt guilty about Jack. But she was thrilled. And she felt guilty about Jack. But she was also thrilled. And guilty about Jack.

Jack took the day off and sat home reading *Sports Illustrated* on the porch, eating his lunch alone and drinking red wine. A bumble bee flew at him and he violently swatted at it with the magazine. Meanwhile the dark red wine spilled all over his light blue shirt. Two women neighbors talking nearby looked over dully as he laughed to himself about the large stain over his chest.

The museum director took Lee to a very fancy restaurant on the west side of town. They ordered vichyssoise with salad, followed by fish and vegetables, and some kind of cranberry-like dish. The dessert was a chocolate mousse with coffee. He talked in monotone about the museum business but didn't seem to have much interest in painting or sculpture. Lee tried to listen attentively but couldn't help looking around at the restaurant help. When she saw a waiter enter the "out" door at the same time that another exited, the crash and the spill made her grin. The museum director looked back disinterestedly at the fallen waiter and continued talking. He spilled nothing, knocked over nothing, and tripped over nothing during the entire lunch. Perfectly poised. Perfectly boring! Lee watched his lips move and thought about Jack.

◊◊◊

Jack had drunk too much wine. He'd poured half of his second bottle onto the kitchen counter before realizing he had no glass. He decided not to risk a glass at all and took the entire third bottle out to the hammock with him. As he left the kitchen he glanced at the photo of him and Lee on the wall under the shelf of pans. He wanted to throw his wine bottle at it, but it was his last one, so he tucked it under his arm and continued outside.

Lee raced home from the museum to find Jack in the hammock. He seemed to be having a conversation with the trees above. Her lips trembled, and a tear came curling down her cheek as she called to him. He stopped talking to the trees and twisted his head to look at her, and the hammock flipped him over onto his stomach.

"I landed on the wine bottle, Lee. Didya see that? I landed on the bottle."

She helped him up and took him inside and made coffee. They sat quietly talking on the couch. And when he sobered almost completely, he agreed to look into that balancing on one leg Yoga thing with her, and they hugged so hard they knocked the lamp over.

# CORRESPONDENCE

Dear Karen,
Life stinks! It stinks so rottenly, so wholly and pathetically that I wish mine would just end without warning or symptoms. I am too chicken to commit suicide, so I'm relying on some unknown person or event to do the job for me. I've contemplated walking through Central Park one midnight, wearing my only suit (although it's a little tight along the shoulders) and pretending that I'm rich. I would carry only Monopoly money (six ones and one five) so that when the mugger notices, he will kill me on the spot (especially if I laugh as soon as he looks at it). That would be the surest way to have someone end it all for me, and I've thought of it constantly, sometimes laughing uncontrollably at the—I don't know, the thrill of it.

I've also considered making a citizen's arrest, maybe marching right up to a Hell's Angels headquarters and telling them to drop their bikes and turn around and try to put their hands behind their backs. I'd be dead in seconds.

I believe I am obsessed with the thought of death, and nothing else has been able to break through these vivid images of total blackness. I believe I will surely carry out one of the above plans for ending my miserable life, and soon. But right now I don't think

I'll be able to, at least not until I get through this mid-term paper that I haven't started yet. There's also a stupid biology test and a history oral presentation coming up. I hate those, so maybe I'll be dead already for that one.

I knew I should have faked that I was mute when I enrolled, but somebody in my history class already is, and two mutes would look too suspicious. I didn't even believe he was mute at first, so I stepped on his foot one day (stamped on it, actually) to see if he would scream or ask me why I did that or something. But his whole face scrunched up and turned red, and a tear soon came out of his eye. Then he whacked me in the side of the head with his palm, and I cried out because it hurt a lot, and he walked away. So he could be a real mute, I still don't know.

Anyway, the reason I've been so obsessed with death, I think, is because of Joann, that girl I told you about in my last letter. She's beautiful, as I told you. She's shy, and smart, and polite, and kind. She's everything I've ever wanted in a girl. For days I followed her around campus and kept asking her out. I knew she liked me, I just knew it. It wasn't until I asked her out the seventh time that I discovered she was engaged. You see, she had politely said, "No thank you," each time, while holding her hand to her mouth. So, being the psychology student that I am, I figured she was saying no but really meaning yes—that she was saying in body language what she didn't really mean with mouth language. You probably don't know about this, but it's one of the universal rules of guy and girl interaction. Always believe the opposite. If a girl says no, get lost, it means yes, please, and to pick her up at about seven that night. If she says yes, it means drop dead or go away. But this one time it was different because when I asked her out for the seventh time, I discovered the engagement ring on her ring finger, and I remembered that it had been there the other six times she'd held her hand to her mouth. What a blockhead I was to have missed it. I'm so

42

depressed. Nothing is good on earth. She is the most beautiful girl in the entire college, and now she's engaged. Darn.

Now you know why I am contemplating Central Park or the Hell's Angels after the first semester (or maybe after the break). Nothing is important. Life has no meaning. Joann was all I lived for—for three weeks! And now she is gone, and I can't function anymore.

I hope this letter isn't too negative, but I feel negative lately, as if the whole world will come crashing down on me (or something similar). Besides what I've told you, I'm doing just fine and I hope you are fine too. Write soon.

Your pal,
Arty


Dear Arty,

Your letter was more positive than the one before it, so don't be so negative. You're positively moving in a positive direction. I'm positive about it. Be positive. There is nothing to be negative about. Negativity is like a vacuum. It positively sucks everyone around you into it, as well as yourself soon after. It positively sucks. In other words, being negative is positively stupid. And if I didn't care about you so much, I'd say that you were being a real jerk for being so negative. So be positive.

As for Joann, whatever will be, will be. Two letters ago you told me she had a bit of a facial tic. Go on that. Keep telling yourself, "She has a facial tic, therefore she is not worth it." Make it your mantra. There are a million girls in the world without facial tics. Think of all of them, maybe all together in one room, and think of that one, that one special girl who will...well, squeeze herself out of that room and come to you with her tic-free face. She may not be so far away. She might be very close to you already. You may be in direct contact with her right now. Think about that. And you can't kill yourself. Who would I write to?

The world is not crashing down on you, Arty, just because of one stupid girl. People care. I care. So quit being such a jerk.

Love,
Karen

Dear Karen,

Your letter had a very strange effect on me. It made me feel like catapulting you to Nova Scotia! Don't tell me to be positive when I don't want to be. And don't you dare call Joann stupid or even suggest she has a facial tic. It was *you* I was talking about, or don't you read my letters carefully. You blink too fast sometimes when you get nervous, which I think qualifies as a tic, and I'll bet any doctor would say so.

I've really been feeling hostile toward you lately. I just thought I'd let you know. I had a dream a few nights ago that a grand piano fell on top of you from an apartment house window. That dream somehow reminded me of the time we were going out together. Wasn't that a ridiculous experience?

I took your advice, though, about there being a million girls stuck in a room and *the* one maybe being in direct contact with me. Just as I read that line I turned around and there was a girl there. No facial tic at all. No rapidly blinking eyes. In fact, I don't think she blinked at all as she asked me for the time. I didn't have a watch but I told her anyway. Later I discovered that I was off by two hours and I realized I'd missed my chance with her. I became depressed again, and still am. And now that I think of it, if you'd never given me that suggestion (about the room full of girls without facial tics), I would never have looked up, and she would never have asked for the time, and I never would have told her the wrong time, and she would never have thought I was some kind of wrong-time-giving jerk or something.

I'm not thinking of death as much as two days ago. Instead I'm thinking of running away, maybe joining a circus somewhere to get away from all girls—*all* of them, and never come in contact with one again, EVER!! (although I will still write to you, of course). The circus is foremost in my mind these days and it rules my thoughts. I haven't been able to find one, though, and I have a psychology exam next week. I hate psychology. It's neurosis this, and neurosis that. Drives me nuts!

Today in the cafeteria I had the urge to bash my forehead with my tray, but the stupid pizza was on it and I was hungry. It's all so *frustrating.*

Dear Arty,

I've been growing lately, I think, and I'm feeling more enlightened each day. I don't know what's come over me but I've been writing poetry and studying music and art and finding out how beautiful it all is. Creativity is beautiful. I'd never thought of it before, really. Whenever people have said "creativity" to me, I've said, "Oh, yeah, creativity," but I'd never taken it seriously until now.

I am convinced that art is the only path to a truly meaningful life, and that love itself is the way by which art should be developed to realize fulfillment. I walk around now with a smile on my face and a song (I know it's corny, but a song) in my heart.

I understand the anger in your last letter, but anger gets you nowhere. I know there is pressure on you with your schoolwork, and that you are not feeling well. So I understand those things you wrote. I understand that you didn't mean them at all.

So now I would like to confess something to you. It's hard to say, so I'll write it instead. I'm in love with you. I've loved you since we were fifteen, and now, five years later, I still love you. You've got so much to give and I know I do. I'm confident that life exists for us, just the two of us, to make it beautiful. I want to make my part of it beautiful, and I want you to know how much I feel that you are a part of the beauty I want in my life. You're everything to me, Arty. My God, I've held it inside for so long, but now that it's out I feel happy. I look at those words, "I'm in love with you," (several lines up) and I am frightened, but thrilled.

I know you will understand because you are so understanding. And a nice guy, too. Please write soon, Arty, and tell me how you feel. Don't hold back. I am very busy lately with my work at school, my job at the child center, and my poetry, but I will be awaiting your letter with open arms (and a letter opener, ha!).

By the way, I love Nova Scotia! Thank you.


Love always,
Karen


P.S. That was funny about the grand piano. I laughed when I read it.


Dear Karen,

That was the weirdest letter I've ever read. You have beaten your own record for weirdity, Karen. And it was a stupid letter too. And selfish. You are one selfish girl, Karen, always thinking about who you love and never once considering who the hell I love. Your letter was filled with selfish gibberish, and so I've decided that when I join the circus our correspondence will be over. All that talk about poetry and art and child centers! I thought I was going to get trapped in La-La Land if I didn't stop reading.

Anyway, enough of that junk. If it's of any interest to you, I've discovered that I'm still in love with Joann. I passed her a few times on campus, and I think one of those times she glanced at me as she went by, a quick darting look before she walked faster. Probably a lot of ambivalence (psychological term you might not know). Anyway, I couldn't believe it. I was so happy. Ambivalence is good. But at the same time, ambivalence stinks because who knows. You know?

But true love, alas, is always the most painful, and it will hurt so much when I join the circus. And alas, she's engaged, so that's another alas. And when I join the circus, I will probably never see her again. So that's a third alas, and maybe the knockout alas.

The most important thing in my whole life is Joann. If only she wasn't getting married. My teeth are clenched, and I'm fighting back the tears, and my stomach is in knots, and my knee has been bothering me. I want to just jump off a cliff, or...if not a cliff, then a ledge, at least, or a curb (because of the knee). My only consolation is in knowing that the most intelligent, most sensitive people suffer the most. Who has condemned me to this suffering? Who is responsible? I shake my fist at the sky but nothing comes of it.

You, Karen, are responsible for our ended friendship. You are yet another friend who I'm forced to break with. And so I say goodbye. Don't write back. I probably won't even answer. My loveless, pathetic life goes on.

Yours truly,
Arty

P.S. I got an 88 on my psychology exam. So I bet I'm right about that ambivalence thing.

# SQUEEZING THE BOOTS

Russ the mechanic said something about a leaking steering rack, and I just looked at him, raising my eyebrows and thinking, what the heck is a steering rack—the image in my mind an automotive-like dishwasher rack deep under the hood below the steering wheel. Long gone were the days my father taught me how to change spark plugs and fix a carburetor and get the starter to work. Now I only knew where the window washer fluid went and how to open its cap.

"How much does that cost?"

"It's under warranty. The dealer has to take care of it."

"That's good."

"Lucky, because it's five hundred dollars to replace."

"That's bad."

So I went to the dealer on my side of town, and while they checked I sat on the edge of a lamppost in the parking lot reading a book. Then the woman at the desk stuck her head out the door, one eye looking straight out at me and the other looking up to the mountains beyond, and she told me I was all set.

"Already? You fixed it?"

She waited until I was inside and she was behind her computer, punching at keys. "There's no leak," she said, not looking up. "It's just the undercoating."

"The undercoating."

"Yes, the undercoating of paint. It happens a lot with this model. It just looks like a leak."

"The undercoating." The image of automotive paint decorating a dishwasher rack came to me.

"So there's nothing to worry about," she said, nodding, and she smiled me out the door, my receipt for zero dollars and zero cents in my hand.

I was happy for a while. No steering rack leak. No replacement job. Just an undercoating. I took my bike out and rode around for a while. Inspection, no problem. Just the undercoating. Just an under coat. Russ had it wrong.

I pedaled past the dealer, hearing the woman call someone over the parking lot speaker. Her face in my mind. Her nodding head. Then Russ, looking at me soberly. No nodding head. The woman's face again. Too much nodding. Russ, having never lied to me, not nodding. Good old Russ. The woman not looking at me. Just the undercoating, she said, not looking. Russ looking at me. Warranty. And Russ not making any money from my car. And (I slowed down on my bike) the dealer not having to spend money on my car. I stopped my bike completely and stood straddling the cross bar, squinting accusingly at the Catskill Mountains surrounding me.

"I think she's lying," I said aloud.

A family-owned garage on the corner was just up the block from the dealer. Fifteen minutes after they took the car in, the wife of the mechanic came out of the garage into the office while I played with an old pinball machine.

"Well, you've got a leak all right. You need to get that fixed to pass inspection."

"It's under warranty, I think."

"It should be."

"The dealer said it was an undercoating or something."

The woman laughed. "Well, bring it back there and tell them to squeeze the boots."

"Squeeze the boots."

"Yes, tell them—" She saw my knit brows. "They're like hoses that keep the dust out of the rack, but steering fluid is getting inside them, meaning your steering rack is cracked somewhere."

"Interesting. So...squeeze the boots."

"Yes, because when they do, the fluid will just leak right through the boots."

On my way back to the car, my mind was filled with nothingness because it immediately rejected the image of snow boots or walking boots attached to a steering rack that looked like it came from a dishwasher.

Often lately I wake up very early, sometimes from bad dreams. That night, I dreamed I had placed a tip for a waitress on a table at an outdoor restaurant. But when I walked away from the table someone crept close to it. I watched him snatch the money, and I went after him, wringing him by the collar and demanding it all back. Others nearby froze, then backed away. I was the maniac, and he was the frightened innocent, and I woke up, groaning, and looked at the clock. It was two-thirty, and I was up for the day.

At the kitchen table I explained it all to my wife, and our seven year old daughter kept asking, "What lady? What dealer? What rack? Boots, what boots?"

I slumped in my chair, glowering out the window.

"Just relax," my wife said.

"I can't when I'm lied to. Remember the builders? I hated those guys."

"What guys?" said my daughter.

"That was five years ago," my wife sighed.

"Still hate 'em. Money stinks."

"Stop it."

"People stink."

"Oh, stop."

"Russ doesn't stink, though. He told the truth."

"See? Just call the dealer back."

"Who's Russ?" my daughter asked.

When the builders were working on our house, it wasn't the nightmares that kept me up.

I took a half-day off from work to meet with the electrician at noon, and he didn't show up. The builder, a short bald man who talked like an escapee from a *Goodfellas* set (curses and all, around my toddler daughter and infant son), called the electrician to yell and curse at him, and I stared sourly at the show he put on.

The siding guy took weeks to fit two strips of siding onto the garage front. "This is all you did the whole day?" I said to him one Saturday afternoon.

"Well, maybe I'll just go hunting, then," he grinned and stepped toward me. Then he laughed to himself and walked away down the block.

"Where are my phone jacks?" I demanded of the builder with weeks to closing. So the electrician had to come back, and when he finally did, he stood against the kitchen sink with arms folded, looking at me. I looked right back at him, but after I went upstairs and came back down, he was gone.

The plumber, sitting with his legs out in front of him like a little kid playing with blocks, hammered through the kitchen concrete and complained that the town code guy required different piping near the laundry room, and who did he think he was.

The builder cursed in front of my wife and kids when my wife wanted a flooring mistake fixed immediately, and I glared at him until he turned away and "effing apologized."

Closer to closing, alone in the car driving to work through the fog, I called out to my father. Dad. I'm not built for this, Dad. I hate this stuff. Why did you go?

I couldn't help but sob, driving between tall leafless trees, because three weeks after the building had started, days before he was to ride up from Long Island to help me look things over, help me plan, help me deal with people like this, he died suddenly of a heart attack. I'm not built for this, Dad, I wept. Where did you go?

"It's the undercoating," the woman insisted over the phone.

"It won't pass inspection."

"Bring it here, then. We'll pass it."

I was silent. Then..."No, I want it up on the lift. I want to see it."

"Sure, you can take a look if you like."

I was to be there in an hour. My wife gave me a worried look on my way out the door. "Are you all right?"

"I want to ride a little first."

"Don't get upset."

"I'm all right. It's the good kind of mad."

"There is no good kind of mad."

I drove off the highway down a path to the river where people sometimes fished. No one was there, so I sat in the car, windows down, with a perfect view of the Susquehanna rolling by fast.

It was the good kind of mad, I insisted to my wife in my mind, just as it was the good kind of mad when, after the builder cursed and "effing apologized," I slowed down the closing on the house, wanting everything just the way we wanted it, making them wait for a change, perfectly happy in our little one bedroom apartment for however long it took. Then the builder came by to warn me not to be unreasonable, that if I delayed the closing—even after he'd promised that he'd have every last nail in place by the weekend—that he'd just stop.

"Stop what?" I said.

"I'll just stop."

I was silent. Months later, when the kitchen ceiling started leaking, because the plumber hadn't tightened something under the upstairs tub, the builder crabbed back at my phoned complaint that I was on my own now, that I had a lot of nerve bothering him on Super Bowl night. The next day I grabbed the plumber at another building site, and he came, embarrassed, and fixed the tub, giving me his card on the way out, which I took and pocketed before tearing it into fours and throwing it out when he'd gone.

I hated all of them steadily, never having hated anyone, really, before. My wife looked on worried when I sat at my desk with my dizzy head down on my folded arms.

And now, for the first time since, years later, that feeling was back. From inside the car, I looked at the racing river and could see myself carried violently along with it if I so much as stuck a toe in. The builders' horrible faces. The man taking my tip money in the dream. The dealer woman's lying eyes.

"Stop it," I said aloud. "Count the people that you love instead, stupid."

I imagined my father, looking as he did when I was a kid, standing by the river.

Where's your camera, Dad? No pictures?

I got out of the car, and he turned to me. What are you doing here? You're going in there knowing the answer already. Just go.

He stood there, confident the way he was about things, and I almost felt his playful smack in the back of my head. Get over there and stop the nonsense.

I walked closer to the river and shut my eyes, listening for a while.

She was there, behind the computer looking at the screen, when I came in glowering at her.

"We'll get you in soon and have another look, but you know, we've had this problem with other models—"

"It's a leak. I know it's a leak," I spat heatedly, pacing away from her and then back. She started to speak— "And when they check the car, tell them to squeeze the boots!"

"Squeeze...the boots," she repeated slowly, looking down at the computer screen.

"That's right, squeeze the boots. And I want to watch them do it." I paced away again. "I'm not paying five hundred dollars for a leaking rack. I've got a warranty." Behind her, a couple of mechanics stopped to look at me. "Bunch of bull," I said to them, then paced back. "Undercoating. Bunch of bull," I muttered to the wall.

I waited in the car, key in hand, smiling at the half-hour wait before going into the garage to ask if maybe it was time they got my car on the lift. A skinny younger man I hadn't seen in the office told me he'd be right out. When he drove my car in another twenty minutes later and got it on the lift, I stood away, not under the car with him, and watched him reach up to loosen something. I saw what looked like small vacuum hoses. The boots.

He loosened, and loosened, and I stepped under the car, looking up, and then both our heads dropped down with the red liquid that trickled rapidly to the ground.

"I would say that's a leak," he said to me quietly.

"Yeah, I would say that too."

Soon I was back in the office, not saying a word, while the woman made the appointment to replace the rack. I stared away from her. Finally, when a couple of the mechanics and a customer were in the office, I asked her, "Who looked at the car the first time I brought it in?"

"That would be John," she answered, not looking up.

"Is he here?"

"No, he finished for the day."

"Well, tell John he didn't even check my car!"

She was polite, this woman, as she made my appointment, so I settled down, thanked her quietly, and left with my appointment sheet.

The angry mask lifted the second I pulled away from the lot. I laughed aloud, passing the cemetery but looking at the sky.

"How was that, Dad? How did I do?" I laughed. "Squeeze the boots. Squeeze...those...boots."

Home was only a few minutes away, but I drove for a while first, circling town in my boot-leaking steering-rack-cracked car, chuckling every once in a while at having known the answer, for once, before walking into a room.

# LETTERS FROM A YOUNG POET

Aug 8, Rome, Italy

Dear Jeanette,
Isn't this neat, my writing "Rome, Italy" on the top of the page like this? Yes, I am in Rome, and I am roaming around lost because that stupid Father Kevin gave me bum directions. I'm supposed to find a convent and a person named Suare Maura. I don't know where this place is or what the hell a Suare is anyway, or how to spell it. Pretty soon I'll need to find a person to ask directions because it's hot and I'm still carrying my backpack. The problem is I don't speak Italian except in curses. Maybe I'll ask a policeman.

It's later. I'm sitting next to the Trevi Fountain. It's too hot here. Hotter than in Deer Park, I don't care what you say. I'm carrying a bottle of water around because that's what everyone else does as they walk. I keep going in circles, so I need a rest. But this water tastes pretty good. It's Italian water that you can't find in Deer Park, except maybe at Bruno's deli on the corner.

I finally found Suare Maura and the convent. A policeman showed me the way. Turns out I'd passed it a million times today. I'm pretty beat. In fact, I'm so tired I've even stopped caring for now about you going off bowling with Al two weeks ago, breaking up with me by bowling instead of saying something face to face like a regular person would.

Still, I am writing to you, and I don't even know why. Maybe because I have to tell you some last words, even if it's from a great distance. That reminds me. I took my two weeks off from the toy store and came here not just to get away from you and stupid Deer Park. I came to write some poems and think about stuff. So maybe I will write a poem now. Maybe a poem about my plane trip—except that all I did was sleep, so that would be a nothing poem. Or maybe I'll write a poem about you...and Al...bowling.

Right now I guess I couldn't write about anything else because I can't think about anything else. You broke my heart, you know that? You and Al can go to hell. Especially Al. Not you as much. But still you.


Aug. 9, Rome, Italy


Dear Jeannette,

I'm sitting on a bench in some park, lost in Rome again. Not as lost as yesterday, but still lost. At least I'm not lugging around that backpack.

I just ordered pizza from a guy in a vending truck. He does nothing but sing and bang on his pizza pans and other pots. It's a bunch of different Italian songs. He has pop eyes. I didn't need to speak Italian to him. He knew just what I wanted when I held up one finger and pointed to a slice.

Would you believe the pizza here in Italy is not like Deer Park pizza? They're small, round individual slices and taste pretty good. I started a poem about the pizza guy, but I couldn't get it the way I wanted it because he kept making so much noise. Here it is so far, so take it with a pinch of salt.

PIZZA MAN
Oh pizza man
You, with your popping eyes
And your round pizza
And your cheerful songs
Banging your pots
Your pizza is the best
Oh, where do you get your bread
With which to make your slices
And do you by chance
Serve Italian ices?

That's all I've got so far. I'm going to try to find the convent again and take a nap. I hope the place didn't move to the other side of the city somehow, because I need sleep. I think I got jet lag.

By the way, I forgot to mention that Suare Maura, who I met last night, is a lady, some kind of nun, not a guy like I figured she would be. She did have a little mustache, and just for a second she caught me looking at it (I could tell), but a mustache doesn't make a lady into a guy. Maybe I can write about Suare Maura after my nap, if I can find the place again first.

I still haven't found the damn convent. Keep going in circles. Do you know that the Italian men here in Rome whistle at the girls and say lousy things to them like there's no tomorrow? They don't even do that in Deer Park. Not exactly. They just grunt, maybe. I know I couldn't whistle and make comments like that to women. That's not right. But look who I'm writing to about what's right.

I'm in a restaurant and think I know where the convent is now because I'm near the Roman Coliseum, which I'm sick of passing. I can't believe I got lost twice in two days. I ordered some spaghetti, which was served to me as linguini, and a whole pitcher of a drink. I think it's beer but it doesn't taste like it.

I thought I was going to fall in the Tiber River on the way back here to the convent because I couldn't walk straight. First they gave me a whole pitcher when all I ordered was one beer. Then they didn't tell me the tip was in the bill, so I paid two tips. I only figured it out in the middle of a stagger. I was so mad I yelled out, cursing like a madman toward the Coliseum. I guess it looked like I was screaming at the ruins, and people passing the other way were looking at me. A bunch of lousy busybodies. The hell with them. And the hell with you too, Jeanette, and tell Al the hell with him too. Two stinkers you are. Four including those thieving waiters at the restaurant.

Tomorrow I'm going to throw these letters in the Tiber River because I don't know why the hell I'm even writing to you, you traitor. Even Suare Maura, who never smiles, looked in on me when I got back tonight, and she served me a hot drink and gave me advanced warning that it was tea. I should write to her instead.

P.S. A rooster here woke me up at 4 a.m. last night. If it wakes me up again tonight I'm going to find him (or her).

Aug. 10, Rome, Italy

Jeannette,

I am on fire with my poetry writing. After the rooster woke me up, I wrote a poem about him called "Elegy to a Rooster." But then after Suare Maura gave me some coffee and cookies (she's not evil like I thought she was at first), I sat down and wrote a bunch of other poems. One is called "Suare Maura." Another one is called "My Flat Feet."

The creative juices are flowing now that I'm in Italy and away from all the ignorant people in Deer Park. I don't mean you, really, but Al for sure. Well, maybe you too. Here's another poem before I get lost in Rome again.

IGNORANT AL
Ignorant Al
Has stolen my gal
She had a heart of gold
But now it is sold
She can keep him
As far as I am
Concerned
And both of them to hell
Can go
And be burned.

Aug. 11, Milan, Italy

Hey Jeanette,

I have one of those train passes, by the way, that takes me any-where I want to go in Europe, but I am only going as far as Zurich where my plane will take me home in a few more days.

Milan is a dark place. Everything shuts down between twelve and two, and even after that I could hardly find a place open to get something to eat or drink. Finally, I walked into a place along a narrow stone road. There was an Italian girl there, and I guess her mother was there. They were both nice. I looked around and finally found water and some bread. Then the girl looked at me and said, "Basta?" I said, "Yeah, uh, basta." And she laughed. What a smile, and what eyes she has. Better than any eyes or smile I've ever seen in Deer Park. Half the girls in Deer Park are so covered in make-up anyway that you'd need to use a paint scraper to get to their regular faces. This girl has no make-up, just beautiful skin and eyes. I bet she wouldn't bowl with Al if someone paid her 100 lire.

GIRL IN MILAN
What beautiful eyes you have
And what a sore spot I got
For a sweetie with a smile such as yours
In a store I can easily spot
From the street
And so, Sweet
May I see you again real soon
'Cause if I don't
I'll have to go back to stupid Deer Park
And howl at the moon

As you can see, Jeanette, this is not no ordinary girl, but a nice one. I'll go back in the morning and say buongiorno to her. Maybe she'll come to Deer Park and live with me and my parents. But then she'd probably hate that. So I'll stay in Milan instead. And be her slave. And live upstairs and slice bread all day and write poems to her.

August 12, a train on the way to Florence

Dear Woe Is Me,
My heart is broke, but it is no fault of the Milan girl, who wasn't there when I went back for breakfast. The whole store was closed down. I kept going back until after two and then at four, but the place stayed closed.
Maybe I'll send her my poems. But right now I'm sitting on the train to Florence with a broken heart.

I stuffed all of the letters to Jeanette into my backpack, under my dirty socks, then wrote a fantasy poem called, "Catapulting Jeanette into Deep Space." But that didn't even cheer me up. All I could think of was the Milan girl, probably hiding from me today, with those store gates down. So I'm stuck with myself now.

August 13, Venice

Dear Myself,

I lasted two hours in Florence. Couldn't find a place to stay. Well, I did, but it was so noisy right outside my window, and all I wanted to do was sleep. So I went to the train station and waited around for the next train to Venice. It wasn't going to arrive until two in the morning, so I sat eating a candy bar out of a machine and reading *USA Today*, which I found a copy of.

Now I'm in a little hotel room, and very sleepy. I tried to sleep on the train but I was so scared that someone would come in and steal my bag that I laid on it. It has my passport and plane ticket in it. And I'm running out of money. I didn't bring as much as I should have.

Venice looked nice from the train when I first saw it, though. Jeanette could have been here seeing it with me instead of bowling with Al in Deer Park. I wouldn't even mind living here except I can't speak Italian and don't know what job I would have. But maybe I could at least write my poems and try to sell them. All I've got at home is the job stocking shelves over there. Big whoop.

The maid just tried to beat my door down. I fell asleep and kept hearing knocking sounds, but I didn't think it was at my door. Then I got up and opened it. It was the maid, mad at me like she knew me, just because she had to change the stupid sheets. I guess it was because I went up too early.

She yelled so fast in Italian that I had no idea what she was talking about. Even if she yelled in slow motion, though, I still wouldn't have known what she was talking about.

MAID IN VENICE
Oh maid in Venice, you are too mad
For no reason
Over sheets
If you were a guy
I would've cracked you over the head
With your cleaning fluid can
And sent you sprawling
Onto your can
And mopped you
Right out the door, far away from me
So I could sleep in peace
Don't you see?

August 14, Zurich, Switzerland

Dear Me,

On the way to Zurich today I watched the Switzerland country-side. It was the most beautiful grass and trees and mountains I've ever seen. Little cottages, too. A beautiful girl on the train was sticking her head out of the train window and smiling as she looked at the hills. I could see her gorgeous blue eyes even from where I sat half a car away. Wow. Just wow. And she knew just when to pull her head back into the train just before the train reached a tunnel. I know if I stuck my own head out the window, even if the coast was perfectly clear, somehow a tunnel would appear and my head wouldn't be attached now as I write this, and my hand would be flopping around useless and unable to hold a pen.

Some more poems I wrote on the train today were: "Girl Stickin' Her Head out the Window on the Way to Zurich," "Deer Park Is No Switzerland," "Jeanette and Al in Hell," "Basta? Yeah, Basta!" and "The Conductor."

THE CONDUCTOR
The conductor of the train
Is always on the move
Even when people are noisy
His stony face won't crack a groove
A bomb could detonate right next to his head
And he wouldn't even know
That he was suddenly dead
He punches his tickets all day
And makes the most of it
Be damned if I know how he stands it
Not to sit

It is later now. I tried to catch up and say hello to the Zurich girl, but she slipped away into the crowd somewhere. Maybe she was an angel.

It started pouring rain when I got to the station, so no one went outside yet, just waited inside or under the overhangs. I stood and watched people running in from the rain, laughing and smiling, all huddled next to each other, and I started smiling, too. And then I was laughing with them even though no one was next to me. Then I felt lonesome. Not for Jeanette. I wasn't lonesome for her at all anymore. Not for the toy store where I worked either, or the crowd at the bowling alley, or any of my high school or other friends, or any other part of my life except for what was missing from it. I stood there smiling with all those strangers, missing everything about life except for what was in it.

I'm in the hotel now and only have about twenty dollars and change left on me, including my plane ticket. Three days to go. On the way here I stood at a bus stop and talked a little to a Japanese girl and her family. They were very nice. They were on their way out to dinner. I asked them if I could come too but they said no, very politely and shyly. Not mean. Not like Jeanette would have, like "Get lost, creep!" Not like that. No, they just smiled and shook their heads and said it was nice to meet me but they'd already made reservations. Just a very nice polite way of telling me to get lost.

JAPANESE FAMILY SAYING NO TO ME AT BUS STOP IN ZURICH

They didn't bow low
They didn't say no
They didn't say "Go!"
They just smiled real slow
They said sorry but we have to go
Nice to've met you, don't you know

August 16, Zurich

I bought peanut butter and crackers from the supermarket today, the cheapest food I could find. Maybe it will last me until tomorrow when I leave. I still need money to call someone to pick me up at the airport. Maybe Uncle Tommy. Lucky I can eat for free on the plane. I think.

I walked all over Zurich and then went into a restaurant and ordered some coffee. They wanted to charge me five dollars for one cup. I told them I didn't want it after all because it cost too much, but the guy behind the bar told me to pay up anyway. I got mad and said no way, it's too much, and started to leave. Then a guy near the door got up from a table and spun me around to go back and get my coffee and pay up. I got madder and moved around him, but he came after me. That's when I got really nervous and pushed at him, and then he slugged me hard in the face, right between my eye and my nose, on the side. Two other guys came and pushed me out the door.

I kept feeling my face all the way back to the hotel, but when I realized I didn't have to pay after all, I laughed about it a little, even though I still wanted to cry at the same time. When I got to the hotel the girl at the desk (another beauty!) was very concerned and took me to the kitchen of the hotel restaurant and put a frozen bag of mixed vegetables on it. She said it always did the trick and should make the black eye go away in about three or four weeks. I told her what happened and she gave me a cup of coffee on the house, and then one to go. The free coffee, not having to pay the five bucks, and her pretty eyes were worth the slug in the face. Made me look tough, too, after I got the chance to take a look in the mirror upstairs. If anyone asks me at home how I got it, I'll tell them I fell out of the plane.

August 17, Zurich Airport

I wrote a few more poems last night. They are called "My Black Eye," "My Dime-Sized Bald Spot," "Al Walks into the Wrong Alley" (narrative poem), and my favorite, "The Girl with the Frozen Mixed Vegetables" (love poem).

This was my last morning in Italy and Switzerland. I said bye to the girl at the desk and vowed to return next year without a black eye and show her all my poems. She said it would be wonderful to see them. I kind of backed away from her, smiling, as I left, not wanting her to get a peek at my new bald spot and change her mind about me. Anyway, I'm only twenty-five, so it will probably grow back by next year. Could be a jet lag side effect or something.

I took the long walk here to the airport and bought two candy bars to last me the wait. I'm lucky I didn't pay for that coffee because I have only five bucks left, not to mention a black eye, a two-timing ex-girlfriend back home, and a tiny little bald spot that had better not get any bigger.

I have to go back to work in two days too, back to that boring toy store serving customers for eight hours a day. So life pretty much stinks.

But I got to write some poems. And I think I'm getting better at it. And I met some nice people, especially those girls in Milan and Zurich and Zurich and Zurich. And maybe someday I'll not be missing so many things that I might not do, and so many people I might never meet. Like now.

# MAKING CHANGE

## Back from Italy

Only two days back from my vacation in Italy and already I am homesick for it, wishing I wasn't going back to work tomorrow at that same old igloo of a toy store—me, twenty-five years old and wasting my life stuck inside from nine to five while there is sunshine outside. Not to mention having this black eye I got in Zurich when I didn't want to pay five dollars for a cup of coffee. I don't want this black eye that people I hate will ask about willy-nilly. I don't want to have this bald spot which I spotted in Switzerland and hope fills in after my body recovers from the time zone change. And I don't want to cross my paths with Jeanette, my two-timing ex-girlfriend who, before I went to Italy, went bowling with my ex-friend Al to break up with me instead of just telling me to get lost like any decent girl would.

## The Parking Lot

It is not crowded in the parking lot. Spaces are all sitting there to be had by just about anyone with a car and a will to park. So what happened when I went into one innocent parking spot on my first day back to work this morning? Some guy with a big bushy blond mustache and a red face was suddenly at my window scream- ing at me because I had took his precious spot. I couldn't hear him because of the radio but saw his mustache quiver every which way like of its own free will. I put my hands up as if to say, "Okay, okay," to him and backed out, almost running over an unsuspecting old lady with a shopping cart first. The guy zapped into his precious space after I left it, but not before he had to lean on his horn when someone else tried to sneak in ahead of him.

I waited in the car, sitting in my new spot, which I guess was unwanted because no one was pounding on my window and screaming at me at the moment. I watched the guy go into the toy store, imagining what I'd do to him if we crossed paths and his back was to me. But soon it was 9:15 already and he hadn't come out yet, forcing me to go in anyway and be late for work. I didn't know why he was taking so long. Probably looking for a bib.

## Sourpuss Sophie

Sophie is the store manager and maybe the queen of all Cov- ington because since she is the manager she gets to boss around anybody within her toy store limits, including yours truly, even though I've been working at the store a lot longer than her snippy self. She was all mad because I was twenty minutes late my first day back from Italy, yelling at me near the break room after I punched in. Then she got even more madder because instead of looking at her while she yelled, I kept glancing around for the guy with the mustache. She moved her twisted face in front of my face to block out my view, so I told her I was not actually late, and that she probably had mistooken the difference in time zones because it was only nine o'clock in Italy. Her nostrils flamed up when I said that, and she grinded at her teeth, so I quickly tried to smooth her over by holding my palms up to her and explaining about my jet lag. That made her stomp away, her heels clacking on the floor. Then as I was putting on my stupid-looking orange vest, she stomped back to tell me I had to work at the register, which I had never done, because Louise was out being pregnant and throwing up all over the place.

## Making Change

While I was in Italy, I wrote a lot of poems, and I was getting better at it and liking it. But ever since I came back, and especially while standing there at the register like a stump, I didn't feel like I could ever write another poem, unless it was about Sophie the sourpuss slipping and sliding on a bunch of loose cans of corn in the supermarket and everyone all around her having a good laugh while she tries to get up amongst them.

I saw the guy with the blond mustache leaving without buying anything (all that parking for nothing). Then two customers were at my register and I had to ring them up. But I was slow figuring out where the numbers were and where the button was to get the change drawer to pop out. Before I knew it there were six people on line, then a seventh—a guy who stood first on one foot and then the other, rolling his eyes every time I punched a number. That made me mad so I kept looking up at him, meanwhile getting even more nervous and slow. Counting out change backward was hard, too, especially with that guy rolling his eyes, and I just couldn't get the hang of it. In short, when he got to me he made some smart comment like, "Where are you working next week, kid?" so when I got hold of his change I put the bills on the counter away from his reaching hand, and I threw his coins in the same bag with the game he bought.

"That's not where it goes!" he screamed.

"Well, that's where it went," I retorted.

He stomped off to find the manager, and Donna, another cashier, elbowed me out of the way and told me I was officially off duty at the register and maybe retired for life.

"I didn't want it in the first place," I told her, but she wasn't listening. I knew that guy had stormed off to complain to Sophie, so I just went in the break room to punch my card. I found a sticky note and wrote to Sophie that I had resigned my position and was sorry about my jet lag.

I headed out of the store, walking faster just as Sophie was calling my name on the all-call phone. I didn't want her clickety-clacking over to me again and yelling in front of everyone. In fact, ever since I came back from Italy, everybody has been stomping and clickety-clacking all over the place. People in Italy just strolled around easily, drinking from bottles of water and taking siestas at the drop of a hat. No one stomped around—except for a maid in Venice after I went up to my room before she could make up the beds. But that's besides the point.

Oh, and also the waiter in Zurich who punched me in the eye for not buying a five dollar coffee. But that is also besides the point. And in Switzerland.

## Hospital Visit

Instead of going home to my crummy apartment, I drove around and wound up at Hecksure Park, which is on the rich side of Covington. It is nice over there and it gave me the opportunity to think things over and ask myself what I was going to do next, since I had had that job for seven years, plus change.

When I was in Italy things weren't so hard. There were new people and places, and the girls I saw and kind of met were nicer and more gentle somehow and in better spirits and more calm. I

**Making Change**

liked being alone and thought about becoming a poet. But of course now I'm sure that my idea was just fool's gold because I couldn't write another poem now even if someone had both my arms twisted behind my back.

From a bench I saw one guy pass who looked almost exactly like that guy from the parking lot. I remembered his red face accenting his shaking blond mustache and his crazy blue eyes. I knew that someday he was going to have a heart attack or something—turning green and collapsing, then winding up in the same hospital room with the guy whose change I threw in the bag.

They'd be there side by side while the nurse went back and forth changing their tubes. Parking Lot would muse despairingly to Coins-in-the-Bag, "I will not never get mad over a parking space again."

"Huh?" Coins would say, laying there.

"I once got mad at some poor guy over a parking space, and it started me on this road to self-destruction. What about you?"

"Well," says Coins, "I thought it was all the heaps of butter I always put on my toast, but come to think of it, I remember once getting mad at a guy because he was too slow counting out my change. I shouldn't have ought to have got so mad. I should have tooken it more lightly. But instead I got even more madder when he threw my change in the bag."

"God, I hate that. That *ticks* me off when cashiers do that to me."

"Yes, but I forgive this guy now. He was really dumb-looking and I felt sorry for him after I got mad, because I think I got him fired."

"It doesn't matter. He had a lot of nerve doing that. He had a responsibility to his customers, and to his fellow man in general, not to throw change into your bag. Besides, he should have been properly trained by an expert. Where did he work at?"

Coins sighs. "I don't know. Toy store, I think."

73

"Same as my guy. He took my space at a toy store parking lot."

"I wonder if it was the same guy."

Parking Lot sits up. "Of course it was the same guy. Don't you see, that guy put us in here. He started this ball rolling."

"Maybe you're right. I always thought it was the buttered toast, but—"

"You're damned right I'm right. We should find him."

"You don't need to curse—or interrupt me for that matter." He presses a button on his bed. "Where's the nurse? I hate waiting."

"I didn't interrupt. And damn's not a curse."

"She's late. That's what ticks me off. She does this stuff on purpose. I see her, you know, smirking, taking her time drawing my blood. I could do it in half the time myself, right now. How long does it take to fill a little vial? Stupid nurse."

"Stop complaining. Anyway, you got the window. Look at me, I'm stuck near the door. I have to listen to other patients moaning. You got a view, at least."

"I got no view. I get to look at one tree branch. One stupid tree branch."

"Better than what I got."

"Well, I was rolled in first. What do you want?"

"I want you to stop being so damn high and mighty alla time."

"You're cursing again."

They would have went on and on, but I decided to get up at last and go to my parents' house and see my father.

## Talking with My Dad

I finally had enough today, I explained to Dad on the patio, and I quit that job, so I need to rest up now and maybe follow the path of a normal everyday poet. I am ready for a big change and hope all my instincts is correct about not wasting my life.

# Making Change

Dad was busy at the barbecue, but he advised me right away, telling me it's better late than never that I quit work and for me to go ahead and join college now and become a writing major or something and study poems like I want to, but I said twenty-five is pretty old, Dad, and maybe I should ought to be a golf caddy like a customer at the toy store offered me a few months ago. They get good tips, I said.

But Dad said, No, stupid. Tips or no tips, get that idea right out of your head because you have a dream to write poems so go on and just do what you gotta do and get the hell out of here.

That made me feel better, so I told him I would sign on the dotted line at the community college and see how I do. It is better than staying stuck here in Deer Park crooning over Jeannette who I have not called since I got back from Italy, nor do I even keep the phone in the jack that much at my apartment.

Dad just worked on his barbecue, nodding his head. He's kind of quiet most of the time, so I got quiet too, sitting on the picnic table bench and missing the people and places in Italy again, remembering how most of the time it felt like I could be calm because the people weren't mean there. I looked up and told this to my dad, but he told me to shut the hell up. He said you are looking in the wrong places. I said I know I am, that's why I want to get out of here, but he said, no. He said, look somewhere *else*, not another *place*. But I said that's what I mean, somewhere *else*. And then he and me looked at each other all mad, like the other one was the wrong one even though we both kept saying the same thing.

## Letter from Jeannette

I got home today and a letter from Jeanette was sitting in my mailbox. I saw her handwriting all curvy and blue on the envelope, and I brung it upstairs with me. I took my sweet time getting

75

changed, boiled my spaghetti at my own leisure, and then yawned and put my feet up on the coffee table before tearing the letter open to see what it said. This is what she wrote to me in her stupid curvy blue handwriting...

Yes, I have broke up with you, but not because of what you think, that I took up with Al. That night I went out with Al only because you made me mad with your joking around about doing nothing with your life.

Now I have heard from reliable sources that you quit your job last week and are indeed doing nothing, so I guess you are getting your wish. Maybe you are perfectly happy to do nothing, just like you were perfectly happy working at a toy store for seven years. At least Al is fixing cars, and even though I am not going with him like you might think, at least he is still coming home at night with grease all over him, unlike you who maybe came home from the store with some box shavings on your shirt. At the most. That is a big difference if you wanna talk about making something of yourself—which after almost a year with you I seen that you wasn't. Especially now that you quit.

So no, I am not with Al now like you think. I am with nobody and have broke up with you because you went off to Italy for no reason on your stupid trip by yourself and have acted like—well, I'm not going to write that word, but it has to do with a horse's dairy air.

Speaking of which, who gave you that black eye in your eye? I heard that, too, from people who know. Not that I really care after what you pulled, going to Italy on me.

Sometimes, to tell you the truth, I do miss you because you have a sensitive streak that almost nobody can see most of the time. But then on the other hand I come to my senses pretty quick when I remember how you get mad about stupid things and then joke

76

around about making nothing out of your life, and never changing, like life is some kind of joke.

I wonder who gave you that black eye, though. Was it some girl you looked at funny? Or did you say something wrong to the baggage rack at the airport? Did you let your eye all alone to get all swollen like a balloon, or did you actually put ice on it right away like a normal person would? But on second thought, I don't care if you tell me anything about your eye or not, so don't even think this is some kinda invitation for you to call me and explain yourself, which it isn't, because I would hang up on you a few minutes after you called, don't you worry.

Love,
Jeannette

When I finished the letter I crunkled it up and slung it against the wall. Then I picked it up again and folded it a few times and flinged it hard, right into the couch. Later, after settling down to eat my spaghetti, I heard the phone ring a few times, so I released that little gray clip from the jack and yanked the phone with all my might out of the wall. Then I laid down on the bed and looked up at the ceiling, and I stayed mad for a long time.

## The Finger

Bad enough starting college for the first time, when I wasn't even sure anymore that I even wanted to go, but I had to have that Jeanette letter on my mind as I drove for my first day of classes. I tried to shake it all out of my head, but what kept getting to me was that I couldn't keep her in the all-enemy department of my mind like I wanted to. I hated her, but I liked her, and loved her, and missed her, too. I felt bad for her, was disgusted by her, wanted to take care of her, wanted never to see her, wanted to yell at her, wanted to spill my guts to her, and wanted to clam up and pretend she never lived—all at the same time. She was all right by me, and she stank to high heaven. It drove me so nuts that I guess I was driving a little too slow, and all of a sudden some guy passed me on St. Johnland Road and gave me the finger right out the window, higher than the roof, as he passed.

I never got so mad in my life, ever. I speeded up and stayed behind him on Route 45 through all the crazy left and right turns, imagining myself catching him at a red light and pounding on his window until I smashed through it, then pulling him out and tossing him onto the road. But when he pulled up to a red light near the college, I just sat behind him, breathing hard, and when he made a left into the college parking lot, I rolled straight ahead and turned into a development. I sat in the car in front of a fancy new house for a while, under the shade of a tree. The street was silent except for the birds, and after I calmed down I frowned at my watch as it crept past the start of my first class, mad at myself, and missing Jeannette, and sorry for everyone, even for that guy, finger and all.

## Brooklyn and the Beach

I am on my way out of town, to Brooklyn, where I found out I could get an apartment near downtown for six hundred per month, and I could leave my car here because who the heck ever uses a car in the city except just to park it? I got almost all my money back from the college after only one day when I seen two minutes after being late for class that it wasn't going to be for me.

Dad didn't say anything when I told him yesterday. He wasn't mad, just worried, I could tell. He frowned, maybe thinking that I will get myself killed for no reason in the city. I told him I was good at minding my own business and I would be just fine (he gave me a look when I said that), and anyway, I said, I didn't want to be stuck in a boring job, or go to college for nothing, and I wanted to meet different kinds of people. He just frowned and looked away. Then he took a long deep breath and said, "Well, I guess you gotta do what you gotta do."

"Yup," I retorted after a little while, and we just stood there not saying anything.

Today I went to the beach and looked at the water, trying to write a poem, but nothing would come out of me. I wrote one title, "You Gotta Do What You Gotta Do," but it went nowhere after that. Some poems might come to me in Brooklyn, like they did in Italy, starting this weekend when I move, but maybe the first one will be about the water at the beach today. It was beautiful, all choppy and white and blue, and it stretched out forever in front of me, all the way to Connecticut.

# LITTLE LEAGUES

After a two inning sampling of my new Brooklyn neighborhood's little league, my old friend Mike, who I was seeing for the first time since our Long Island days, wanted to sit behind the backstop with the rest of the crowd and study their behavior, but I frowned and looked away, hoping he'd leave it alone, that we'd go over to the basketball courts instead and get into a three-on-three, or watch the old men play bocce.

It wasn't only the parents yelling for "John-ny! Domin-ic! Sammy!" and "Jo-seph!" or their impassioned entreaties to the umpires to open their eyes, to put their glasses on, to change their contacts, to get into their rocking chairs, to get new wives, to turn to religion: it was the screaming at the coaches to put that kid in or get that kid outta there; and it was the sarcastic comments—the "Good catch, kid," or the "Hey, look what I found!" or the "You want my niece's glove, kid?" that made me glare at them all. It was all of that and Mike's increasing antsiness to go sit in the stands and have fun among those cursing fools that made me blurt out, "I hate this crap." A thick silence for a few pitches, and then Mike went into the stands by himself. I didn't follow but turned away and drifted to Smith Street, picking up a coffee at the pizza place and then crossing the basketball courts toward the bocce court, hating that crap, hating it furiously all the way there.

The men on the bocce court took turns rolling big balls toward a tiny one, sometimes slowly to get close, sometimes hard and fast to knock the big balls free. They spoke only Italian to each other, and a couple of them nodded to me when I sat at the far end and took the lid off my coffee.

Three of them played against another three, and one of them immediately reminded me of my Uncle Emilio, five or six years dead now. This man seemed serious, but he took it well when he made a bad roll and the others razzed him. He played the part of the beleaguered one, shrugging his shoulders and smiling wryly at a particularly bad turn. They rode him, and I smiled, sipping at the coffee. They were all so quiet and serious during someone's turn, but then there was an explosion of kidding and shouting and warnings and advice and boasting, all in rapid Italian.

When I was ten, eleven, and twelve, Uncle Emilio greeted me upstairs whenever we went to my grandparents' two-family house in Queens. He talked to me about the Mets and we watched baseball together. He spoke some English and some Italian and made jokes, wearing such a serious expression that I had to pay close attention to get the humor. He didn't take baseball so seriously, but he loved it, and he knew I loved it too.

The gestures and expressions of that beleaguered bocce player reminded me of Uncle Emilio; and another man (I took a gulp of coffee and peered at him) reminded me of someone too. From late childhood, maybe. Teen years. Long Island neighbor...Pete Spiezio's father. A lost defeated look in his eyes just before he rolled a ball clicked the memory into place. Pete's father had once stood behind the dugout, his fingers gripping the chain link fence, watching with the same lost gaze while Pete dug out his black shoes that teammates had buried in the dirt under the bench.

I looked at the sky, at a plane high above, remembering that joke Phil Moran had played on Pete. I was twenty-two or so and out for pizza with friends. With Kevin and Nick and maybe with Mike himself, the last time seeing him before then. Phil Moran showed up, bought beers to go with the pizza we'd ordered, and cancelled the sodas. He told us the joke that he'd played on good old Pete Spiezio, slowly leading into it and wearing that easy-going sardonic smile of his, not getting to the punchline until we were already laughing.

He'd sent a letter to Pete and his father, he told us. Used New York Mets letterhead. Really official. The letter invited Pete and his father to spring training in St. Petersburg so Pete could try out. They'd heard about his skills, the letter said, and their scouts couldn't wait to see Pete play.

Of course Pete and his father flew down, paying for the plane tickets themselves. We all laughed, imagining what their faces looked like when puzzled looks or dismissive replies greeted them. Some secretary giving the letter right back and sending them on their way. The long walk out of the ballpark. The long drive to the airport. The long plane ride home. And their disappointed, embarrassed faces—especially the lost look on the face of Pete's father. My laughter turning into a weak smile.

I sipped the last third of the coffee, not smiling now, watching the men play bocce. It was either a good roll or a bad roll, or a near miss, and all the while they rode each other mercilessly and took it well. Mr. Spiezio's look-alike, quieter than the rest, smiled weakly at their jokes or at their feigned anger.

Late college, on the way to the train station, I met Pete coming from the library, balancing a stack of eight or nine books in his arms. I glanced at the top group of books about self-improvement or body-building, and Pete, in his booming voice, suggested I read a few of them. He held one and then another out to me. I could borrow any one of them, he said. Really. But I told him I was late for the train.

Pete in the weight room in high school, pumped up and grunting among other lifters. Friends and I had wandered in from gym class. Mike was there too. Nick elbowed me. Do you believe this guy? Pete finished a set and nodded an emphatic hello to me and moved on to bench pressing. Focused. Knew he was being watched.

One of the bocce players knocked someone's ball off course or something, and there was a collective shout from the men, half of them cheering and the others roaring no. One of them shook his bent head, and they all walked up the court, pointing at this ball or that one and ribbing each other. I grinned.

It was all playful ribbing, but the boys in those days hadn't ribbed Pete. The invitation to the Mets' training camp was no rib.

Pete's father (I looked at his replica again) had died a few years before, leaving Pete living alone in that big house, his mother having died when he was a toddler. I stared at the chain link fence beyond the bocce court.

Gripping the chain link fence, Pete's father had stood behind the dugout after that game in junior high school. Pete was in ninth grade, and the eighth graders, Morris and Devlin and Carson and McCormick and Pops, sat on the bench digging holes with their spikes, gradually merging their holes into one big one. When Pete was in the field, they buried his black shoes.

Pete played second base regularly, and I was a seventh grader, playing the second halves of games in the outfield. I watched them bury the shoes, then quake silently with laughter when Pete came into the dugout and looked around, first curiously, then more urgently. I looked away, back out to the field, before I heard Pete scream, "Where are my shoes! Where are they?" And the eighth graders broke out with suppressed laughter, looking out at the field, not at him. "Where are they," Pete screamed.

"We don't know where your stupid shoes are," one of them said at last, and they broke up again.

That was no rib. I watched them laugh and hold it back, laugh and hold it back, and I watched Pete grab a bat and stand near the other end of the dugout waving it up and down with one hand, glaring at them.

It was no rib, and Pete could do nothing but take it and wave that bat, then hurry to the on-deck circle when the coach yelled at him.

They had no idea where his stupid shoes were, they insisted, angrily sometimes, all the way to the end of the game, saying it to the coach too after the coach, laughing too, finally told them to cut it out and give the guy his shoes.

Later, when the game ended, I lingered while Pete searched furiously, but there was only dirt and a wood bench to search, so I stood next to him and toed the dirt under the bench. The eighth graders looked back at me from near the bus as Pete dug frantically, and that's when I noticed his father, standing behind the dugout, gripping the chain link fence. He looked on quietly, lost, while Pete dug out his shoes and emptied them of rocks and dirt. Pete paced the dugout, his shoes in his hand, and he didn't say anything or look at me.

They were about to start a new bocce game, and it seemed that Uncle Emilio and Pete's father were on the same team again. They were to going to roll first, determined this time to undo the lousy game they'd just played. The others needled Uncle Emilio playfully because he was giving some serious advice to Pete's father, and Pete's father smiled and rolled. They roared about his good shot or bad shot, I couldn't tell which.

Yes, Pete's father, maybe, told Pete to start lifting weights after those boys buried his shoes. Still, in high school the kids laughed at the bulked-up Pete when he got off the bus, because he ran full speed, wearing his black shoes with white socks. He ran awkwardly, all the way down Jason Lane, elbows pumping.

Sitting in the front seat of that bus in my mind, I wondered about Pete and why he hurried home. To see his father, maybe, and have a catch, or just practice alone. Maybe to play private imagined baseball games, the way I often did then, secretly, as crazy about baseball as Pete was. Quieter about it, though. Not laughed at. Only secretly loving it, not hurrying to my baseball glove after school but taking my time and reaching for it casually later, stone-faced, throwing the ball off the chimney only when I knew no one was watching. The games inside my head, contests with myself, a whole world inside me, one that I liked.

Pete's hero was Mickey Mantle, but he was crazy about the Mets and sure he would play second base for them one day. I only hoped silently, but he was positive about it and often said so in his booming voice. So they tortured him—Morris and Devlin and Carson and McCormick and Pops.

"Mickey Mantle's a drunk," they taunted him on the way to practice one day, as we clicked in spikes through the back of the supermarket parking lot. "The Mick's a drunk, Petey," they said, and Pete screamed, "He's not a drunk! He's not a drunk!"

They laughed, and laughed harder during practice when I misjudged a fly ball hit to me in centerfield. I went back on it at first and then came in as Pete ran out from second. The ball dropped in front of me, and I threw wildly to second base to cut off the runner, but Pete couldn't duck my throw in time and the ball caromed off his head and into left field. The runners circled the bases and the guys in the infield fell down laughing. Pete dropped to one knee, holding his head.

"Sorry, Pete. Sorry," I said, hurrying over to him. He blinked rapidly and nodded. He was all right, he said, and ran back to second, but not in a straight line, weaving everywhere. And in between hoots, one of them, Pops maybe, shouted to Pete that he was running just like his hero, Mick the drunk.

I stood, looking for a garbage can for the coffee cup. One of the bocce men nodded to me, and I nodded back and threw them a wave. I liked them. I liked the way they played. I knew I'd be back.

Crossing the park, I could still hear the little league game. The screaming and the cursing became louder and closer before I veered away at last and headed home a block away. Maybe Mike was still there, sitting among the crowd behind the backstop and enjoying his study of them. But I'd studied enough, I was sure.

# ORCA (A MADCAP THRILLER)

Accidentally, not on purpose at all, but only accidentally, I happened to harpoon this stupid wife of a whale, and her husband gave me a look like I did it on purpose or something. He looked at me deadpan-like, so I gave him a deadpan look right back before he sank back into the water, slow and purposeful. To tell you the truth, I haven't got time to worry about a whale's feelings; my business is on the sea, and no whale is going to give me "the look" and scare me onto land. Like he can really do something to me. Like I'm really scared. It's really very simple. He's in the water. I am on a boat. He can't think. I can think. I'm a movie star. He's a fish—animal, mammal, whatever. To be safe, to be completely safe and smart, though, I went back to land and picked up a couple of extra harpoons and my best pal and his wife to bring along on my sea adventure...for company.

Well, he has done something after all, this whale. He has killed my best friend's wife, played by Ann Margaret. As she was brushing her teeth near the edge of the stern (a rookie boating mistake), this wise guy of a whale shot up out of the water, scaring her into falling overboard, the toothbrush still in her mouth and a perturbed look on her face. My best friend, played aptly by Boris Karloff, called to her in a cryptic voice, and the music got weird. In short, the whale ate old Ann, slowly, in time with the music, and watched me the whole time. As he munched, he watched me in particular, and not Boris. What have I to do with anything? Boris married her, I didn't.

Later, after dinner down below, Boris vowed over wine, still cryptically, that he would kill that crazy whale if it was the last thing he ever did. But I told him he was not going to kill that whale or any other whale and it was only the wine talking.

"You're right," he muttered after a while but said he was still mad about it.

That crazy whale has been stalking me and Boris for the past three days. We don't know if he's toying with us or whether all our meetings and battles in the open sea are just coincidences. Boris keeps crying and screaming at him, "Where's Ann? Where's Ann?" Is he for real? Get over it.

The whale's attacks and the bad vibes from the audience have gotten me to a point where I had to put in a call to my old pal Bud Abbott to make an appearance in this film. Of course, Bud could not possibly help kill a whale, but frankly I'm in a bit of a pickle because the audience hasn't liked me since I killed the stupid thing's girl. Maybe if they latch their sympathies to a straight man like Bud they won't end up feeling completely ridiculous pulling for a whale to eat me.

We picked up Bud at the docks but waited until we were safely out to sea and the whale had attacked us three times before we told him what was up. Because he is a straight man, he couldn't get panicky and go to pieces on us. Instead he kept yelling things like, "Waddya you guys think you're doin'!" and "What's the big idea!"

◇◇◇

90

## Orca (A Madcap Thriller)

My best pal Boris is no more, and now the whale has really gone too far. It was no big deal his eating Ann, but today I shook my fist at the whale as he spat half of Boris back onto the ship and tauntingly blew water out of his blowhole at me. We'd all been sleeping peacefully below when Boris woke up, telling us that Ann was calling to him. "Are you crazy? Go back to sleep," grumbled Bud. "Waddaya think this is." But Boris got up anyway, sure that he had heard Ann calling him. Then Bud and I sat up in bed because we heard her, too, and we just looked at each other. By the time we got up on deck (too late because Bud had to put on his suit and tie and couldn't find his hat), we heard Boris gurgling, and we looked in time to see the whale munching on him. I already told you the part about the whale spitting half of him back on deck and spouting water at me, so I won't mention it again.

This morning, Bud and I vowed either to get even with the whale if it's the last thing we did (my idea) or go to the Copacabana (Bud's). Bud was spooked because the whale had impersonated Ann Margaret, but I told him it was just a fluke and to stop worrying.

"It's not a fluke, it's a whale. Waddaya talkin' about, a fluke!" He smacked me in the back of the head, but I wasn't in the mood for a routine and was thinking things over.

In the cabin after dark, we heard some eerie music coming from outside, and then Boris' voice. For a while we pushed each other toward the stairs to be the first to have a look. But then we decided it would be smarter, because it was a bit chilly outside, to stay in the cabin and not fall for any more of the whale's impersonations.

After we wolfed down our breakfast, Bud and I decided that it would be best for both of us, as well as the sensitive audience, not to allow ourselves to be eaten. We decided to set sail immediately for land and head for the Copa. "Revenge is sweet," admitted Bud, "but you oughta see the goils at the Copa."

Not that I was at all scared, but I decided to cut my losses rather than to be cut in two, so that I will be in shape for the sequel. So big deal, the whale wins this one—my two friends to his one wife. Anyway, Ann wasn't even a friend. She was a pain, and brushing her teeth off the stern was the dumbest move I ever saw. Any whale in his right mind would have taken advantage of her in that situation.

And Boris? You can't blame the guy for following after the voice of his dead wife, but still, it was the second dumbest move I ever saw, and the oldest trick in the book, impersonating a guy's dead wife in order to kill him too.

So Bud and I docked and lit out for the Copa. We kind of smirked and then laughed to each other as we looked back at the water and didn't see any sign of the whale.

After dinner and three or four Pina Coladas, Bud was already out on the floor dancing up a storm, but I was more reserved, slowly sipping my fifth Pina Colada and eating my pie. All in all, it had been a crazy week, and I was glad it was all over. "A guy makes one mistake, killing a whale's wife," I remarked to the waiter when he came over to clear the table, "and then the whale gets all mad about it." The waiter looked at me and nodded as he swept up the crumbs. "What was I supposed to do, let him eat me? It wasn't my fault, and he had to go and be a jerk about it."

The music suddenly changed from Benny Goodman to something slow and creepy. Bud stopped dancing and we looked at each other. Then the whale himself crashed through the Copa's windows, flying past the bar, through some diners and dancers, and heading straight for me. I heard Bud yell, "Waddaya think you're doin!" as the whale continued to roll along the floor in my direction. I was too woozy to move and just sat there as the creature came at me, mouth open. It stopped just short of my table and could go no farther along the old hardwood floor.

"See what I mean," I said to the waiter, "he's being a jerk." But the waiter had run off and so had everyone else, and I smiled to myself, figuring I could get away without paying the tip.

# NEVER TRUST A POOL SALESMAN

Last spring my neighbor Frank, who at the time I considered just a stick-in-the mud uneven-mustached divorced Professor of Something, walked by my house, as usual, with his dog and two daughters. One of the daughters is eight and the other six, and they're a lot nicer than their father. I've even told him as much to his face several times recently, but he just says, "Yeah."

Anyway, I was working in the garden that morning. My boyfriend Travis had taken a ride to the state university where he'd landed a possible sweet deal with the college on new pool equipment. At least that's what he told me. So later Frank was walking past, and he said, "Hey Mindy, where's One Dimple? He can play at the park with us." I rolled my eyes, refusing to answer him. He called my son Billy One Dimple because when he smiled only one side dimpled up. I turned away from him to pull a weed, but he walked right up onto the lawn. "Listen, Mindy," he said, "you should read the local newspaper once in a while."

I looked back. "What for?"

"What kind of jalopy does your boyfriend own?"

"Jalopy?"

"Okay, heap then."

"None of your business."

"You're right," he said, and walked off.

I dismissed his nosiness as jealousy, but once inside I scanned the paper with a frown. There was nothing strange on the first three pages except rising taxes and closing businesses and a murder. But then on page four there was a little story about a college woman who'd been run over by a Comet. "Light grey heap," said the paper. "The car and the driver both left the scene," said the police captain.

At dinner that night, I took a long look at Travis. We had been living together for more than three months, but I didn't even know what his favorite color was, or his mother's name. I felt myself pouting. We'd talked about getting married a few times, but then he always started laughing and kidding around and tickling me until I couldn't stand it, so I stopped bringing it up.

As he ate his meat loaf that night, I looked at his face. He chewed slowly and stared disinterestedly at the table cloth. Once in a while his eyes darted over to me and then he continued to chew and stare at nothing.

"What're you looking at?" he said finally, biting into another chunk of meat loaf.

"How about we take a ride into town tomorrow? Spring is here. Maybe we can get some ice cream."

"Fine."

"Did you see the newspaper today? Some girl got hit by a car."

"What girl?"

"I don't know what girl. She was a college girl."

"People get run over every day. Don't read the paper if you don't want to read bad news."

The next morning I bought the newspaper again. Another woman, near thirty, had been hit. No witnesses this time.

"Let's take your car for the ice cream today," he said to me when he came down for breakfast. "My fender's rattling."

96

Billy wanted a black raspberry cone, as usual. I had a chocolate one, and Travis said he wanted blueberry with a cherry on top. The guy behind the counter looked a little younger than me, maybe early twenties. Dimple on his chin.

Billy and I started in on our cones before we even sat down, but then there was a commotion back at the counter.

"Where's the cherry? Where's the damn cherry!" Travis screamed.

"Oh, I forg—"

Travis flicked his wrist and the blueberry ice cream landed with such a plop on that boy's face! I'll never forget the sound of it. The poor guy was too shocked to do anything except let the ice cream slide down. As the ice cream hung on his trembling chin and then dropped to the floor, Travis pushed me toward the door and demanded the keys. He floored the car all the way down Hudson Street, up the service road, and then down Beaver Street. He went seventy in a thirty mph zone right past the state trooper building. When we reached the driveway he stopped so short that we all pitched forward. Then he slowly turned the key.

"Okay, guys, let's get into the air conditioning before the ice cream melts," he said cheerfully.

Another newspaper report the next day: this time an old woman had been hit, at night—about the same time that Travis said he was at the library looking up books about bromine. He had taken my car to work that morning, so I went into the garage to look at the fender. There were rust-colored stains on it.

That afternoon Frank walked his dog alone past my house. I looked out the screen door at him but he wouldn't look over.

In the evening, I asked Travis about the stain on the fender, kind of casually, and he laughed and said he hit a deer. "I'm fine but that deer really went flying. You should have seen it!"

I looked up a private detective, a man named Bracken. I wanted Travis followed. I had to know if he was the one. The detective was the only one listed in town. He was a big man with a red face and I doubted he could keep up with anyone at all, but I sat across from him and told him what I wanted.

"I didn't think private detectives even existed," I said to him at first.

"They appear more in fiction than in real life," he said. "But I'm real. Here." He crossed over to me. "Feel my muscle."

"No, I couldn't—"

"Feel it, just the biceps."

I squeezed a little.

"See?" He sat down again. "I get two hundred dollars a day, plus expenses, plus snacks, plus shoe money if I wear out my soles in a chase."

After a couple of weeks of not hearing anything from Mr. Bracken, he reported back to me at last. Travis, he said, did absolutely nothing out of the ordinary. Nothing. He went to work, he went out to lunch, he went back to work again, and he went back home. I told the detective that was impossible, that he had to be mistaken, that he was taking my money, that he was just sleeping on the job or something, that more women would be killed, that he was a thief.

"I'm not sleeping on the job," he said, all insulted.

"Well, is this all you have for my two hundred dollars a day?"

"There are a couple of women, actually, that he'd been involved with in the past. Here are their names." He handed me a paper. "He cleaned both of them out after he left them, so I would watch myself if I were you."

"Gee, thanks, you're a great detective."

◇◇◇

The next morning I went out to visit the first woman on the list, a woman named Clare Bean. Clare was very nice and invited me inside for a coffee and we talked about Travis. I told her about the ice cream incident and about the newspaper accounts and the stains on the car. She nodded the whole time.

"Has he left you yet?"

"No. He still comes home."

"When he leaves you, change the locks. Actually, that might not even work. After he left me, he started sneaking in at night and taking things. First it was my new pack of Lender's Bagels. The next night the butter. The night after that the kitchen table was gone. I still don't know how he got it through the door without making noise. So I changed the locks. After the locks were changed, I came home from work to find my couch gone. Then my coffee table. Soon it was just little things. My toothpaste, my can of Raid." She paused. I was terrified. "Caulk," she added.

"How do you know it was him?"

"How do I know it was him? Of course it was him. Do you know, he tried to run me over while I was planting a dogwood in the yard! All of a sudden my own car was barreling toward me, his smiling face behind the wheel. I dove into the empty lot, like Mannix, at the very last second, and ran to a neighbor's. He just kept driving across people's yards, right to the street, and then he was gone. I never saw him again. Honey, you better be careful."

Next I went to the second woman, Violet Heaving. She was a pretty brunette, but didn't seem too bright to me. She told me the same thing about missing precious items, one by one, until she was cleaned out.

"Why didn't you call the police?" I asked her.

"I did. They didn't do much. Wrote down everything that was missing. Soon *everything* was missing. I had an empty house."

99

"Did he ever try to run you over?"

She looked thoughtful. "Well, noooo, but one time he ran over my hand with a wheelbarrow while I was kneeling in the garden. I was sure at the time that it was nothing. Well, actually, the barrow part, the metal thingy, the round section part, hit me in the head first, and I guess as I was falling to the ground, you know, the wheel continued right over my hand. Wow, that hurt. My hand had a tread mark on it and everything."

"What about the conk on the head?"

"I don't remember if that hurt. Anyway, if you garden, just be careful, that's all. And if he leaves, move. But don't ask him to leave because he has an unpredictable kind of a temper, now that I really think about it."

I thought about the ice cream.

The day after I talked with Violet, Travis didn't come back home. He had my car. I was left with the murder weapon, which I drove noisily around town wearing sunglasses.

Soon enough, I returned from work each day to find something else missing: my snow blower was gone, then my rake, my lucky Mets hat, and the thimble from the Monopoly game we once played (he was the thimble). My toaster...gone. Then the kitchen sink. It was always something.

Finally, the news stories of hit-and-runs stopped, and so did the break-ins. I junked the murder weapon and had to buy a new one. I was broke and broken-hearted and jumpy the rest of that spring and into the summer. I even put up with Frank's wisecracks and started letting him come over to visit for dinner with his kids. That's how scared I was.

Then one Saturday, Frank and I went to the ice cream shop with his kids and Billy. I kept seeing cars that looked like Travis' car, so I was nervous and weepy and sick to my stomach. Frank didn't

100

know what to do except tell me that everything would be all right and order ice cream.

Then I spotted him—that horrible Detective Bracken, sitting on a corner stool holding a big cone with a cherry on top. He saw me too and grinned and came over.

"Hello, Detective," I said, only glancing up briefly.

"Yeah, hi," he said. "Hey, Frank, thanks for the shoe money. I just got these at J.C. Penney's. Take a look." He made us look down at his stupid new loafers.

Then I realized and looked at him.

"That's right, Missy. Frank here hired me to follow your old boyfriend, and to protect you, and he signed my worn-out shoe sole clause, which you were too cheap to do."

"All right, Bracken," Frank said.

"I watched the whole time while he cleaned you out."

"Wait, you watched and didn't do anything?" I was furious.

"Let me finish, will ya? I would have arrested him if he'd killed you, but nothing happened, so relax."

"Are you finished?" Frank cut in.

"Oh, I get it," Bracken said. "Family moment." He started to turn away but then came back, and Frank and I both rolled our eyes. "Anyway," he said, but before he went on he took a huge bite off the top of his cone, so we had to wait while he sucked at it and grimaced at the cold on his teeth. "Anyway, you don't need to worry anymore about your serial-killing boyfriend. He is off to another city looking for more victims."

"How do you know that?" Frank asked.

"Because I know, that's how. It's my business to know where killers go and stuff like that."

"Well, if you'll excuse us—" Frank began.

"I'll tell you what else I know," Bracken said, shoving the entire rest of the cone into his mouth and then spitting little cone pieces

101

on our table as he spoke. "I know that your new boyfriend Frank here is *not* a serial killer" (people started looking over because he was talking too loud). "I can tell right away if a guy likes to run over women, or if he don't. It's my job to know that kind of stuff."

"Well, good for you," Frank said.

"All right, all right, I can take a hint. I'll leave you two alone. I'm off to find your old boyfriend."

"And arrest him, I hope," I said.

"Arrest him? Now how am I going to make any money or get new shoes if I simply arrest the guy?" he snorted, and then ambled out the door at last.

I don't know why but I got weepy all over again after he left. Frank didn't know what to do, so he got up and ordered another cone. I couldn't tell if I was with him now because I cared for him or because I just needed a non-serial-killing boyfriend. I was so confused.

Frank, back with his cone, bit out the bottom of it and noisily sucked out the ice cream from that end. I smiled at him, teary-eyed. Then the guy at the counter called out to him, apologizing because he'd forgotten to put the cherry on top. Frank told the guy it was no big deal and not to worry about it, and he went on sucking at his cone.

That's when I really started bawling. I was actually boo-hooing. It was awful. Frank stopped sucking at the cone and looked at me. Then, slowly, he reached for my hand, and I reached for his. We left and headed for the park with the kids, but before we crossed the street he warned us back, reminding us that real people like us could never hope to be like Mannix, the great TV detective, who dove out of the way of bad guys' cars, or rolled with ease over their hoods. I wailed at him to shut up, please, and not ever make that joke again—or order a cherry on top of anything, even in kidding. He promised.

# THE FLIP SIDE

When he was fifteen Glen promised his father he wouldn't quit anything again after he lasted only a half-hour as a busboy in a restaurant and another half-hour picking strawberries.

The restaurant job at Isabella's Restaurant in town had actually lasted ten minutes, not a half-hour, because he was trained by a senior bus boy first. When the first customers walked in and sat down at a lone table, the waitress handed Glen a basket of bread and told him to take it over to the customers. He hesitated inside the kitchen, then went over and whispered to the waitress, "Which table?"

"Which table?" she cried, and he winced. "Which table do you think?"

He looked out at the couple sitting next to the window and lingered as the waitress rolled her eyes and stomped away from him. Then he gently put the basket down, took off his busboy smock, and slipped out the back door.

At Hatch's farm, Mr. Hatch taught him how to pick strawberries. It took ten minutes for Glen to learn the technique of bending over, fussing with the leaves, finding the strawberries, snapping them off, and dropping them into a container. He was to be paid five cents for each container he filled. But after fifteen minutes, he felt hot, and bending over like that was killing his back, so he lay down in the row of soil. He picked and nudged his body forward, and picked and nudged his body forward again. Then he heard a shout from Hatch's house. It was Mr. Hatch.

"What the hell are you doing?"

Glen stood, holding up an almost-full container of strawberries and pointing at it.

"What the hell is that? You're picking like a goddamn Chinaman!" Mr. Hatch roared, walking over to show Glen how to pick the damn strawberries again. He shoved the container back into Glen's hand and walked away.

Glen didn't move until Mr. Hatch had rounded the corner of his house; then he carefully placed the container of strawberries on the ground and walked home.

The waitress had been a nasty thing, and stupid Mr. Hatch was prejudiced against Chinese people, but his father didn't care. He'd better not quit anything again or else, he said, because once you start quitting, it gets too easy to quit. It becomes a habit.

Now Glen was nineteen, and he'd just finished his second year of college. An agency in Covington had gotten him a summer job at Damico's Ice House, the largest distributor in the county. Every freezer in every store seemed to have a bag of Damico's ice in it, though Glen never noticed until after he worked there.

He took a bus from the train station to the ice house, which was on a side street just off Main Street in Covington. It was an enormous plant with two large trucks backed up to a dock. Inside, a machine churned loudly next to busy men, some around his age, some older. Mr. Damico, a completely bald man wearing all khaki, brought him into the plant and told him he was to work at the conveyor belt. Someone named Keith, who worked at the belt too, showed Glen how to pick up the bags of ice as they rolled along the belt, then place them into a larger bag. Four ice bags were to fill a larger bag, and the next guy had to staple it together and carry it to a palette. When the palette was loaded with four bags around and eight bags high, it was to be wheeled into the back room. The front room was kept at forty degrees, but the back room was at ten. Glen looked outside where it was a sunny ninety degrees, and he started work.

A little man they called Angel, who wore what looked like a train conductor's hat, worked at the head of the belt. Ice poured at intervals from a spout into a bag that Angel held open. He would then guide the bag through a tying machine, drop it onto the conveyor belt, and open another bag for the next interval of ice. A set of empty bags was clipped right under the spout, and all Angel had to do was pull one open. He was very fast, and he made it look easy. Behind the belt, next to Glen, a huge bin of ice formed into cubes and tumbled their way toward Angel's spout.

After about a half hour Mr. Damico appeared at the entrance, his face red. "Relay, relay, relay!" he spat out. "It's as easy as ABC!" The guys around Glen worked faster. "I got a list as long as my arm!" Damico screamed, and went back to his office.

Glen looked outside at the gently stirring leaves of a tree across the street, thinking of a dream he'd had the night before. A girl he didn't know was in his dream, and she leaned back into his arms. He said to her, "Nothing matters except you here like this." She said the same to him. Then the dream shifted and there were people after him, intent on killing him. They cornered him in a room, and he escaped only because he knew it was a dream and woke himself up, his heart beating fast.

Someone behind him shouted because he'd missed a bag, and Mr. Damico was at the entrance again. "Move, move, move! Relay, relay!" he roared.

Break time was ten minutes long, and Glen raced with everyone else to a corner deli where he bought coffee and a roll with butter.

Everyone sat under a tree. One of the men who worked in the back paced in front of them, lisping, "Free Manson. Free Manson." Glen looked wide-eyed at Keith who only shrugged his shoulders and smirked.

One guy named Mike was shorter than the rest but tougher looking. He did most of the talking during the break, and soon Damico was yelling at them all that break was over and that they'd better move it, move it, move it. Glen still had half of his coffee left, which he gulped down.

Before noon a different guy with a thin blond mustache was stapling bags for Glen. He leaned over and told Glen he wasn't bagging right.

"I am bagging right," Glen said, glancing over nervously. "I'm putting them in the bag."

"You're not doing it *right*," the guy said, and Glen looked open-mouthed at the blond's smirking face.

"Yes, I am," he said, continuing to bag. "Look, I am putting these little bags of ice into this bigger bag. I am bagging them right. You see?"

"Bag them then, and shut up," the blond said, pushing at his shoulder, and Glen stopped bagging to face him. He knew there was no avoiding a fight.

"What's your problem?" He felt his voice shake, and the guys hollered at him from behind to pick up his ice bags.

Glen only partially blocked the blond's punch to his cheek, then rushed the blond, who was lighter than he expected, ramming him into an almost-filled palette of ice. They wrestled to the ground before hearing Damico's booming voice, and a bunch of the others pulled them apart and yanked them up.

They told Damico that Gutman, the blond, had started it, but Damico ordered Glen and Gutman to the back room where they had to chop ice off the floor.

At first, Glen and Gutman chopped far from each other, using heavy steel poles. Soon, Gutman edged closer, still chopping. "Sorry, man," he said.

"All right," Glen said, feeling at his cheek and trying to move his stiffening jaw from side to side.

At lunch he sat outside on the dock against a wall, away from the others. His mother had packed a pepperoni sandwich for him, and he pulled it out of the bag along with a book by Rilke. His jaw ached and his fingers were frozen. He couldn't open his mouth very wide so he took small bites as he read. His mother had also packed an apple, but he just shook his head at it and shoved it back into the bag.

There was a commotion at the other end of the dock. Some of the guys were shouting to a girl around Glen's age as she walked by the plant. They hooted after her and made obscene shooting gestures. Frowning, Glen watched her rush past as they continued to holler. He thought of his dream the night before, and felt some vague promise of a future with a girl like the one in his dream. "Nothing matters except you here like this," he remembered, looking at the swaying trees.

Mike was standing in front of him now, his face serious. Glen stiffened where he sat against the wall as Mike motioned to him with his chin. "You like reading, man?"

Glen looked at his book, then back up at Mike. "Yeah."

Mike stood above him, nodding. "That's good. That's good." And he walked away.

The sun was just beginning to warm his numb hands when Damico shouted that lunch was over. It had only been a half hour. Glen closed his eyes before getting up. The walk into town was a short one. The bus for home came every twenty minutes. But he couldn't quit. This was his summer job. College money. No choice. He got up and remarked to Angel on the way inside that he should have taken a job at an ice cream shop instead. Angel didn't laugh or say anything.

Glen was back working at the conveyor belt, and Gutman was on the palettes. The noise of the plant became deafening, and Glen began talking aloud to himself.

"This is the most boring job I've ever had. How can anyone do this for eight hours with these little dinky breaks? I hope that whole palette falls on Gutman. That was some dream last night, some dream." The guy stapling next to him couldn't hear him or wasn't paying attention.

Someone relieved Angel for a while, and things slowed down with a new bagger. The others yelled at the bagger to hurry up, so he got mad and walked away.

"You go. Go," Glen's stapler urged. "You can do it. Go."

Glen hurried over to Angel's station, flipped the switch, and started bagging. The first shot of ice went right through his hands, ice and bag crashing together to the floor. The second shot of ice came before Glen could get the next bag open. He opened it in time for the third shot, but couldn't get it through the tying machine and had to try three times before he got it tied. Meanwhile four more shots of ice poured at his feet. Guys were either yelling or laughing when Damico stormed in and shut the machine off. Glen looked down at the pile of ice that covered his feet and climbed halfway up to his knees.

"What the *hell* is going on in here? You!" He shoved Glen out of the ice. "Get in the back room and start chopping. Where the hell is Angel?"

"In the bathroom," someone said.

"Go pull him out."

Glen walked into the backroom and chopped ice until the next break, then ran with the others to the deli. He was one of the last to get his coffee and roll, wolfing down the roll and curling his frozen fingers around the coffee cup. The nut still lisped about freeing Manson, Gutman still looked like he wanted to fight, Mike still did most of the talking, and the rest of them howled crudely to every girl they spotted.

Near five o'clock Damico came in to scream at everyone that he still had that list as long as his arm, that he didn't need any of them, and that they'd all better relay, relay, relay the last goddamn ten minutes or else. Angel set the machine faster and they raced to five o'clock, but they still had to fill the last palette before they could punch out. They didn't get to leave until ten minutes after five.

"Pretty good day," Glen said to Mike on the way down the dock stairs. "I only got thrown into the back room twice, and my face punched once."

"See ya, man," Mike said, looking gravely at Glen.

Glen pulled the Rilke book from his bag as he walked to the bus stop. He wondered if the agency would have a different job for him when he went back the next morning. He'd take anything they had besides this.

He threw up his hands when he couldn't cross the street in time to catch the 5:20 bus, but rather than wait at the stop for the next one, he walked along Main Street, finally wandering into a little book store. A young woman, a few years older than Glen, maybe, was at the register.

"Hi." He held up his book. "Do you have anything by this guy?"

Her face brightened. "Oh my God, Rilke. Are you reading that for school or something?"

"No, just on my own."

"That's great," she said, and led him to the shelves along the back wall. Glen had to hurry to keep up with her. "Are you a big poetry lover?"

"I like stories more than poems, but I like this guy." She browsed a bottom shelf but shook her head over any sign of a Rilke book.

Then she looked up at him fully. "Oh my God, what happened to your face?"

"Oh. Uh, punched."

"Punched?"

"It's nothing. I get punched every day."

"You're bleeding."

"Not anymore. There's just blood there."

"Come in here."

He followed her to a back room that looked like a miniature living room. There was a table and more shelves filled with old books. She turned on a faucet at a little sink near the window, and he splashed his face and took the dry towel that she handed him.

"You really need ice," she said.

"It's too late for ice." Then, realizing, he felt at his eye and laughed. "I should have thought of that before."

She was gazing at him seriously and he grinned, embarrassed. "I have something for you," she said.

"No, no. I'm all right."

"It's not for your face." She led him out to the back wall shelf and browsed. "This." She pulled out a book. "Take this. You'll love this one."

He took a thin black hardcover from her. It was *Eugene Onegin* by Pushkin.

"No, I can't—"

"It's used. You can have it."

"No, no."

"Or borrow it then. My father's the owner here."

Glen looked at it. "Really?"

"It's such a great book. What a writer. Oh my God."

"Didn't he die in a duel, though?"

"Yes, but you won't die in a duel if you read it."

He pressed at his sore cheek. "Thanks. I have to catch my bus."

She led him to the front of the store, and he watched her hurry behind the counter to serve a customer.

"Let me know what you think," she called after him when he reached the door.

He hurried across the street for the 5:40 bus, but he missed it. Then he leaned against a building in front of the bus stop, flipping through the Pushkin book and reading individual lines of print. "Wow," he said. "Wow."

When the six o'clock bus approached from the end of the block, he promised himself that he'd make the 5:20 the next day. He nodded about the idea of not quitting, of never quitting anything, and he wondered about the flip side of things: the girl leaning against him in the dream; the trees bathed by the sun across the street from the ice house; the beautiful girl hurrying past Gutman and the others at lunch time; the bookstore owner's daughter who'd noticed his punched-in face. Mike's random respect.

He wouldn't quit. He'd read Pushkin or Rilke or maybe Chekhov during his breaks, watch the leaves stirring on the trees, revisit his dreams, and stay completely away from Angel's station.

# THE VENTRILOQUIST

His name is Sal, and him and his wife—my crazy sister Rita—live downstairs from me and my wife, but you'd think their apartment was just some rest stop since they know their way around our place easier than their own and have become experts at cleaning out the refrigerator. And since Sal couldn't get no job for a long time after they got married, they saved on grocery, electric, and phone bills, and the wear and tear on their carpet by doing most of their time with us.

While Sal had no job, him and that stupid ventriloquist dummy of his would be up in my apartment all the time, not just eating my food but making Marian and Rita laugh like hyenas. Every time the dummy said something they laughed.

At the dinner table one evening, I said, "What the hell are you laughing at? All it said was pass the salt."

"It's the way he said it, that's all," Rita said.

"Well," I said, "what does a dummy have to be sitting at the table for anyway?" Then the dummy turned his head to me and said, "Dummies have to eat too, you know, bub."

The girls started laughing again but I screamed that it wasn't funny and brought my plate into the bedroom to eat my dinner in peace. Stinkin' hunk of wood.

For months Sal freebooted off me until finally landing himself a job at a bowling alley.

I said to Marian, "What the hell kind of hit is a ventriloquist at a bowling alley going to be?"

"What do you mean?"

"How are they going to hear his jokes over them bowling balls and pins?"

But she said, "You always look on the dark side. He has got himself a nice job and you are still against him."

"I will always be against a moocher and a bum," I said.

"Why tell me?" she said. "Why don't you tell him?"

"Maybe I will," I said.

"Who's stopping you?"

"No one."

"So?" she said.

"So what?" I said.

"So go ahead," she said.

"So shut up," I said and walked away from her. I hate when she does that. She acts like a little kid sometimes and you can't argue with her about nothing.

That night at dinner everyone was quiet. I say everyone, not just Marian and me, because as usual my sister and brother-in-law and that dummy was eating our food.

"You know," I said finally, yawning. "Maybe I will go see this great performance tonight. I bet the only way you get any laughs is if you perform in the bar and everyone is all juiced up. Or maybe you two girls will be the only ones laughing."

"You might be right, Quasimodo," said the dummy to me (and the girls were already laughing). "Maybe you should come up on stage with me and we can take turns talking..." Sal had to stop and take a couple of deep breaths. "...to confuse the audience," the dummy added.

114

"We'll see how funny you are tonight, buddy!" I yelled over the girls' cackling.

So that night me and Marian was on our way to the bowling alley to see this great act, and I was thinking, my sister doesn't know her ass from her you-know-what. I was going to say this to Marian, or say, He's a bum, or, I hope he bombs, but I clammed up instead.

"What are you so quiet about?" she asked.

"I am having a moment of silence for my freedom," I grumped, and she looked at me crazy like she didn't know what I was talking about.

The bowling alley was packed with only bowlers, and not one comedian was in sight, so I said to the man at the desk, "When does that stupid show start?"

He looked at me blank. "What stupid show?" But then he remembered. "Oh, that. It's in the bar."

I turned to Marian. "See? It's in the bar," I said, but she looked away and pretended like she was deaf.

So we went in, and of course no one was laughing and the place was dead like a funeral parade was passing by. "What did I tell you, he's a bum," I said, but Marian wasn't even there. I was talking to empty space because she was already running over to sit with my crazy sister.

I stood in the back and watched for a while, just shaking my head. Sal spotted me, and it looked for a minute like he got something in his eye before he and that dummy started talking back and forth all about me, razzing me about my big feet and my corns and bunions and pimples, and then getting personal, talking about once that I got dressed up like a woman. So at that point I yelled right out to the audience, "I never dressed up like no woman. I just squoze into my wife's jeans once by an accident."

115

There was a big uproar of laughter from everyone, and they all clapped for a while. Then my brother-in-law and the dummy laid off me but started talking about how the dummy and my sister (Sal's own wife!) was having an affair. Dopey Rita was laughing hardest of all as the dummy kept making Sal jealous.

"Hey," I screamed, "that's my sister you're talking about!"

Everyone laughed and clapped, even the bartender, so I beat it out of there, steaming. Outside the door, some big bowler guy came up to me and said, "What the hell's going on in there—we can't concentrate on bowling."

That's how it went for a while. Rita and Marian kept dragging me to all the shows, but after a while I got tired of hearing people laugh at nothing, and besides, it was always the same jokes about me or my sister, and every time I opened my mouth to say something back, all those drunks would crack up like I was part of the act. So I stopped going.

Then one night after dinner and after Sal and the dummy went back downstairs to change clothes, Marian and Rita nagged at me about going back to the alley to watch.

"What for?" I said. They couldn't think of nothing, but they followed me into the kitchen, and Marian said, "Well, it's Friday night and it will be a high class crowd."

"Nice try," I shot back at her, my mouth full of pound cake, "but I'm not—you're not as dumb as—as I look."

That shut them both up. They just looked at each other, and that was that, but after a few days I begun to notice that Marian wasn't speaking to me. After about a week I couldn't take it no more, so I asked her what the hell was the matter, but she acted like she was deaf and dumb.

I seen that our marriage was at the crosshairs, so to speak, and I stood like a stump in the kitchen while she went about her business. So finally I said, "You know, I feel like going to see good old

Sal do his routine at the alley tonight." She pretended like she didn't care one way or another, but pretty soon she got her coat, and then in the cab she was talking my ear off so much that it felt like we just met and were going on a first date all over again.

When we got there I told her to go in first because I wanted to bowl a few frames and maybe I'd miss some of those jokes about my sister and that jiggle-o-dummy. She kind of growled, but in a romantic way, and said fine, but she ordered me to hurry up, that she'd have a seat waiting.

I bowled a few frames near a bunch of guys who were playing two against two. They seemed like good guys so I started talking to them, and pretty soon one of them said, "At last it is quiet here at the alley ever since that ventriloquist act in the bar started going down the tubes."

"What do you mean?" I said, and another piped in with, "It used to be a big hit, but ever since that brother-in-law character quit the act no one's into it no more. Lucky because we couldn't hear ourselves bowl." They laughed and I felt my face get red.

"Now maybe him and those two women of his can get out of here and let us play in peace," the first guy piled on before they turned back to their game.

I wandered over to the bowling racks and rolled a few balls slowly back and forth over the rack, the steam building inside me. Two women of his, two women, I rolled, burning up, and then I turned and stomped into the bar.

"The party's over, Sal," I shouted. "I told you—you and that dummy ain't funny!" Everyone laughed and I swatted my hand at the whole place and went to the bar to get a drink.

Pretty soon Sal and that dummy began talking about me again, and it was like a riot in there. I didn't look up once, though. I sat there quiet while they both talked about how as a teenager I was kicked in the head by a pony, and that once I thought the mailman was Mitch Miller and kept asking for his autograph, and how as a kid I kissed the caterer at my grandmother's funeral because I thought she was just another relative. All those fools lapped it up and kept looking over at me for my reaction, but I kept my face like stone and drank. Those hyenas still loved it.

When the act was finally over and we were on our way out, we heard that the bowlers were complaining again, but I said, "Out of my way," to anyone in front of me until we all got outside. Sal wore a big smile and said his jokes were so good that they wanted him for another month at least. Then we piled into a cab for home.

I stared out the window while the girls in the back with me yacked up a storm. Sal and the dummy sat up front until Sal threw him back to the giggling girls. After they finished fawning over him (especially Marian, who I looked at like she was a weirdo), they sat him next to me. I sneered down at him and muttered, "Shut up." Then I sneaked an elbow to his head.

Before we knew it, the sober driver was yelling at us to get out because we had arrived home and didn't know it yet. We all spilled out, and I was about to shut the door when I saw the dummy still sitting there alone in the back seat. I almost said, Come on, let's go. But instead of saying something to him or picking him up, I shut the door and the cab sped away.

Sal took only a few steps toward our building before he cried out like a wild man, "The dummy!" People walking by looked at him funny. I shouted out real convincing with, "Sal, you jerk, where is he?" And the two girls cried like they just lost their son.

The next part of the story is pretty sad, I guess. Sal went back to the bowling alley the next night and tried his act with just his hand. He drew a mouth on his thumb and made it move like it was talking while he did his ventriloquist thing. Neither my wife nor me was there, but my sister was and she told us the crowd got ugly

118

because he didn't draw no eyes on his hand, just the mouth on the thumb. "We want the dummies!" they chanted, and finally booed him off the stage.

"See?" I said later to my wife. "His own wife now sees what a bum he is. Without no dummy or no one to joke on he's nothing."

"Shut up," my wife said to me, her face all twisted up and our first date feeling like a dream. "It's your fault in the first place. The dummy was next to you in that cab. I'll bet you left him in there on purpose."

"I did not leave him nowhere," I said to her, but she came right into my face.

"What are you laughing at?"

"I ain't laughing," I said.

"You ain't now, but you laughed when I said you left him on purpose. You *did* leave him in the cab, didn't you?"

"No!" I said, acting mad, but then I let out some compressed laughter.

I don't want to tell what happened next with details. It's just that she didn't believe me and kept walking away from me, so I stomped out and wandered the streets. And when I finally came home late she wasn't on no speaking terms with me again.

She didn't say nothing to me for two days, so I decided that, to save my marriage, I had to find the stupid dummy. I went to cab companies all over the city, but the only thing those creeps would answer would be, "No one here except us dummies," or, "No dummies here, except maybe Wilson." Or they'd say, "The manager has just stepped out, maybe we can help you." Wise guys.

Soon Rita, who at least believed that I didn't leave her husband's precious dummy in that cab, told me that Sal had quit the act, and while roaming around the city he'd gotten himself beat up pretty bad. He was sitting on a bench in the Staten Island Ferry station calling people idiots behind their backs and even right into their faces without moving his mouth. But then he made a mistake. He said it to some big guy while the big guy stared right at Sal's face, confused. But instead of quitting while he was ahead, Sal repeated it faster, finally slipping up and saying it the regular way when someone bumped into him. The big guy looked surprised and socked his jaw.

So Sal was in the hospital and I was thinking, I will never admit it but this is all my fault. I roamed the city, looking into every store and close into every person's face for signs of the dummy before buying a grape juice and sitting out in the park, slumped and sour on the bench. Some kids passed by across the park from me, a few teenage boys and a girl, talking in all kinds of different voices and laughing. And that's when I saw him, sitting on the tallest boy's arm, while they took turns insulting each other in crazy voices. I got up slow and snuck after them from behind, and while they pulled at him for a turn, I yelled, "Hey, that's my dummy!" They all laughed at me and gave me fingers, but when I made like I was going to run after them, they ran and threw the dummy off to the side, into the mud.

I took him over to a diner near the park and cleaned him up and sat him down in a booth across from me while the waitress brought me a big dinner. "You owe me," I said to him just as the waitress got to me with my order.

I carried him over to the hospital for Sal to see. He looked up at me with sad eyes, and even though his jaw was wired shut because it was busted he still said thanks, and then he asked me if I knew of a good way to commit suicide. I said no, I did not know of no good way and for him stop talking crazy because Marian was mad at me because she thinks I left the dummy in the cab on purpose and that he had to pull himself together or she'd never speak to me again. I told Sal to hurry up and get better and get another job ventriloquisting somewhere, and I promised to go along to all his acts and let him joke on me again.

That's it. Marian finally spoke to me again but only after Sal got better and got another job, which to tell the truth, deep in my bones, has made me quieter with her and not as mad at Sal. It all feels kind of permanent, too. A guy can only take two or three silent treatments before he gets quiet too, even if he doesn't want to be.

Sal and the dummy are back together, closer than ever, and the dummy is as good as new except for a little mud in his ear. I don't care about their razzing me anymore because half the time I'm not even listening. Everyone down at the pool hall loves his act, especially the pool hustlers and the gang members—although a few weeks ago during Sal's act a bunch of gangsters got shot up just as they were laughing about my pimples. Everyone ducked, and when we got up a bunch of the gangsters was laying on the ground and the dummy had a hole going through the two sides of his neck; but Sal uses that now by making the dummy drink something and it all comes squirting out the sides and everyone loves it.

So except for that one shooting it ain't so bad at the pool hall. At least there is conversation and violence and hilarity there, unlike at the homestead.

# WANNABES

Ray and Eugene, who were cleaning the upstairs carpet at the local dealership, ignored the shouting outside until the lobby window shattered. Glass was everywhere, and the bloody-headed driver bawled out of a Camaro's window something about taking the goddamn car back. Salesmen squeezed themselves shivering into one small office, but the boss stood his ground and glared at the driver, who sped backward over crushed glass into the parking lot, then spun and swerved his way to the turnpike.

The boys, high school seniors, continued their steam job uncertainly, asking each other what the hell just happened, when the boss strode in. "Stop working." He turned to a young man in a suit who stood in the doorway. "Who is that guy, a friend of yours?"

"He's not my friend."

"Who is he then? Where does he live?"

"I know where he lives but he's not my friend."

Ray and Eugene glanced at each other.

"Come back next Saturday, boys," the boss told them, and they lugged their steam machines past him and tried to hurry down the stairs. "Did he buy that car here?" they heard the boss bark to the man in the doorway.

"He bought it here but he's not my friend."

"Where's the phone? Get me the phone."

"It's in your office. He's not my friend."

From Herman's Pizza, Ray called his girlfriend Carrie and told her all about the nut who'd crashed the Camaro. "I swear these guys are like Mafia or something."

"There is no Mafia," Carrie told him mildly, and Ray rolled his eyes to Eugene, who shrugged. "You watch too many movies."

"You weren't there. This boss guy, he gave the death stare to his worker and said, 'Tell your friend he's dead.' He scared the crap out of us." Eugene frowned out the window.

"It's just an expression. Kids say that to each other in the hallways all day at school: 'You're dead.' 'No, *you're* dead.' 'No, *you* are.' It's a common expression. You said it to me just last—"

"You don't believe anything, do you?"

"I believe what I perceive in my own brain and with my own eyes and ears. Hey, save me a slice, will ya? I'll be right ova."

In the school hallway on Monday morning, a crowd of students talked excitedly about what happened, but it wasn't news to Ray or Eugene. Ray tried to tell the gossipers that he'd been there and seen it, but big Lenny and the others talked over him about that connected, mobbed-up, hit man hothead who hadn't liked his Camaro's upholstery and crashed his car when the dealers wouldn't take it back.

"I heard he waved a gun," big Lenny added.

"No, there was no gun," said Ray. "We were there, we—"

"And then the boss told him he was a dead man," big Lenny went on. "He pointed a finger at him, like shooting a gun."

"No he didn't," Ray said, and Eugene shook his head and strode away.

"Do you even know who that boss is?" said Lenny. "That whole dealership's a front."

"Holy crap," someone said.

"Everyone knows it but you," Lenny went on. "That's why I don't even walk by there. I don't want to wear cement slippers."

Ray scoffed. "I was there, so I know."

"That guy's such a dead man. He's dead. He's a dead man," Lenny said.

"Holy mother," someone else said.

"He's not dead," Ray said.

"I know he ain't dead *now*," said Lenny, scoffing "I didn't mean it illiterately."

Back to finish their rug cleaning job the following Saturday, Ray and Eugene wouldn't even look at each other or talk much. All their steam cleaning movements were hurried, and when they had to empty dirty water and refill the steam machine tank, they hurried that too, splashing up water and cursing under their breath. When they were almost finished, Eugene told Ray he couldn't wait to get out of there and order a couple of slices at Herman's. "I've had enough mob talk to last me a lifetime," he said. Then that same worker from the Saturday before stood in the doorway again.

"Hey, you two recover from last week? You both looked scared to death." He laughed like a horse. "You scared of broken glass?"

Ray and Eugene shrugged as they packed up their machines.

"You know what happened after that, don't you?"

"No," Ray said, and Eugene drifted over to the window

"My boss made a phone call, that's what happened. You know what making a phone call is, right?"

"Well..."

"Sure you know. Anyway, it's not like in the movies, where you tell a guy face to face to kill another guy and give his name. You call a guy who knows a guy who knows another guy, and that guy is told who to hit."

"Oh," Ray said, and Eugene nodded staccato-like down at the steam machine hose he was trying to clip around the tank.

"Guess what happened, though."

The boss roared something from the hallway, and Ray and Eugene jumped.

"Guess what happened," the worker repeated. "That guy with the Camaro—Mike's his name—he got the call. He got that very call, and when he heard the details, he put two and two together and knew it was himself he had to hit." The boss bellowed, closer, but the worker ignored it and horse-laughed again. "He has to hit himself, so now he's like—on the run, man—from him*self!*"

The boss threw open the door. "What the hell are you doing in here? Didn't I tell you to work the floor?"

"Sorry, I'm coming." He winked to Eugene and Ray. "Tell your friends," he said, and rushed out of the office, past the glaring eyes of his boss.


From the back seat of Ray's car, Big Lenny tried to tell the story of Mike the hit man, that he had—"in point of fat"—killed himself, but Eugene cut him off.

"I don't want to hear it."

Carrie, sitting up front with Ray, yawned, "There ain't no Mafia. What're you, kidding us, Lenny?"

"But listen, it's funny," Lenny said. "This Mike the hit man, you know, he was ordered to kill himself. Get it? You see the—what's that word? The irony—yeah, the irony of it."

"Look," Eugene said, "all I care about is going to Nancy's party and meeting some different people for a change. That's where we're going and that's all I want to know."

"There ain't no Mafia," Carrie said, looking out the window.

"Oh yeah? Then why did he do it?" Lenny said. No one answered. "I said why did he do it?"

Eugene blew out a breath. "Do what?"

"Why did he kill himself, then? Because they found him just yesterday. He jumped out of a motel window."

There was a long silence as Ray made a right turn into Nancy's development and eased the car to a stop two blocks from Nancy's house.

"Who told you all this?" Ray said quietly, his hands still on the wheel, while Eugene fumed at the trees outside.

"Friend I know."

"What friend."

"Guy I know, from the dealership."

Ray thought for a while. "Does he laugh like a horse?"

Lenny thought. "Yeah, a little bit."

"So he jumped out of a motel window," Ray said flatly and looked at Carrie, who knit her brows in answer.

"Yeah, down on Route 9, that's right," Lenny said.

"Well, how do you frickin' kill yourself jumping out of a motel window?"

"Look, that's all I know. The guy's dead. It's in the papers too, so it's true. He was splattered all over the parking lot and everything."

Eugene glowered out the side window and shook his head. "You're a stupid ass," he muttered.

"Hey, don't yell at me, Eugene. I already got an earache. I slept on one side all last night, and it's bugging the holy living crap out of me—all the way to holy hell."

Nancy's party was filled with intellectuals—most of them college kids and maybe only half from Eugene's own neighborhood. Eugene found himself drifting away from Big Lenny and Carrie, and even Ray, and he struck up conversations with girls and guys who were art majors and philosophy majors and lit majors. He wondered where he'd be in a year or five years, away from his neighborhood, with new people like these. There were so many other possibilities on the way, he thought as he talked with the others, and he ached for escape. After four or five drinks he felt a deep buzz and sat in a beach chair next to a girl whose name was Wilma, then Willa, then maybe Wawa, and across from him was a guy name Shaboo or Shampoo or something. Shampoo was a lit major who went on and on after finding out that Eugene knew who Scott Fitzgerald was.

"*Gatsby* was a horrible book," Shampoo said. "*This Side of Paradise* was his masterpiece."

Eugene shrugged. "I like Gatsby. Old sport...I like that."

Shampoo spoke in monotone about Gertrude Stein and Sherwood Anderson and Hemingway and Faulkner and T.S. Eliot and "that whole ridiculous twenties crowd," and Eugene sat back, blinking away sleep. After his next drink, he raised his eyebrows to Wawa when she leaned her shoulder into him a little.

"I'm a *Gatsby* guy," Eugene offered at last when Shampoo stopped droning to take a breath. "Anyway, I just like to read."

Shampoo smirked. "Gatsby and his fake mobster friends...a bunch of wannabes. Do you know that I've been playing pool lately with a *real* hit man?"

Eugene tipped his head back against the chair, and saw the top leaves of the darkened tree above him. "Really."

"Sure, I play at Bradley's over near the college, and I met this guy, a really fascinating guy. We play about once a week." He paused importantly. "And he told me offhand that he's a hit man."

Eugene leaned forward, away from Wawa's shoulder, and stared at Shampoo. "He told you that?"

"Why not, that's his job. He's just a regular guy."

"No, he's a hit man. He kills people."

"It's not like that."

"He could kill you."

"It's not like that. Work and pleasure are separate in this guy's world. He wouldn't kill me. We're pool buddies. That's the whole beauty of it."

Eugene looked around for Ray but only saw Lenny swaying near the barbecue.

"Beauty of it? He kills people. I wouldn't play pool with anyone who kills."

"How do you know who you're playing pool with?" Shampoo said, and Wawa's head lolled. "But at least with this guy, it's his job, it's all up front, and the people he kills are bad anyway."

"I kind of admire him," Wawa slurred.

Eugene struggled to get out of the beach chair, pushing off Wawa to get up and away from Shampoo's knowing smirk. His chair tipped over, and Wawa almost tipped over herself, but he didn't stop. He gave one last sweeping look at the blurred crowd in the yard, ducked out of the front gate, and crossed the lawn. The sounds of the party dulled behind him and were soon replaced by the silence and the darkness of the tree-lined development. He circled on foot for over an hour, unable to find the turnpike. No matter what kind of route he tried, he found himself back at the party house. In the yard again, he smiled weakly to Carrie who sidled over to him.

"You look all ready to go," she said.

"I'm ready." And when Carrie was quiet, he added, "I'm ready to get completely out of this crazy neighborhood, totally out of here. College can't come fast enough."

"You got that right," she said.

"Since I was a kid all I've heard is this stupid phony mob talk. I'm sick of it."

"There is no mob, and there ain't no Mafia," Carrie said, and waved across the yard to Ray.

"Amen. Thank God you don't believe that crap."

"I refuse to believe that crap," Carrie said. "Ever since they threw my Uncle Nelson in the river when he couldn't make his payments, I refuse to believe any of it. I swear on my mutha."

# WITH DOLEFUL VEXATION

## After the Harbor

My first date with Carly was ice cream and a walk to the harbor to watch the boats and the old men fishing off the docks for no good reason. All went well. She even looked at me with goo-goo eyes at one point as we parted for the afternoon near her block.

"Thank you for the ice cream, and for the walk," she said with skillfully concealed glee.

"You are very welcome," I answered magnanimously. "Maybe we can do this again sometime."

"Or something else," she ventured bashfully.

"Perhaps we could take in a basketball game, then," I wondered brazenly, out loud so she could hear me.

"Yes," she replied hoarsely, looking curiously at her left elbow. "Call me, then," she added with averted eyes.

"I most certainly will," I said, waving my arms histrionically. "There is a game on Wednesday night, and perhaps we can take the train."

"Oh, that sounds nice," she said soporifically. "But now I need my beauty sleep," she added with half a smirk, "because it is already half-past three."

"I will call you with the details," I nodded officiously. "And we will have fun, especially on the train," I added with a fake elbow jab, which she dodged nimbly.

"Sounds great," she replied gigglingly.

## Ma

"Why won't you stay for dinner," scolded my mother with deeply furrowed brows.

"Because I am taking Carly on a second date," I replied smoothly. "We will likely have hot dogs at the game."

"A second date and already gallivanting off to Madison Square Garden?" exclaimed my mother accusingly. "She is only eighteen and you are old enough to be her father."

"I'm nineteen, Ma," I answered with brusque correctness.

"And twenty next month," added my mother simperingly.

"Ma," I said, with rising irritation, chewing on a few Ritz crackers with restrained hunger, "she will forever be one year and three months younger than I."

"Not at this rate," blurted my mother with convoluted rationality. "What are you taking her to, the circus?"

"Of course not. The Knicks game," I answered, spitting out little cracker pieces despite a great effort to stifle them.

"Don't say I didn't warn you," she remarked cryptically, her apron catching fire briefly on the stove.

## Her Parents

Before our glorious train ride, I was compelled to meet Carly's parents whilst picking her up, so I pressed the doorbell with ill-concealed trepidation. When her youthful sister answered the door, I ventured onto their costly carpet.

"Carly, it's for you!" screamed her sister, full-lunged.

Her father came out of the bathroom one beat later, and he gave me a bleary-eyed and bloated nod, or maybe, I thought with compassion, he still had to go.

I smiled toothily when her mother stuck her head out of the kitchen doorway, but withdrew in terror when she screamed up the staircase apoplectically, "You better be home by eleven, or you're dead—you hear me—dead!" Carly was at this point in time running down the stairs, and she ignored her mother and bloated father. "Let's go," she said to me moodily. Then she glanced waywardly behind herself to her mother. "We're going to the movies," she lied, with great aplomb.

## On the Train

"You still owe another four dollars," the conductor informed me with ghastly eloquence.

"What do you mean?" I replied with fake stoicism.

"You don't buy at the station, it's a two dollar surcharge," he answered with real stoicism.

"But..." I looked to Carly and then back at the conductor. "I won't have any money left for hot dogs," I whispered to him with conspiratorial alarm.

"Four dollars," said the conductor with razor-sharp apathy.

Carly, noting my extreme predicament and reluctance to fork over this seemingly arbitrary penalty, reached into the miniature handbag on her lap.

"I've got it," she said wearily, and handed over four dollars to the stone-faced conductor.

"Thank you for riding the Long Island Railroad," he said with a straight face.

◊◊◊

## The Game

While I purchased our costly hot dogs, Carly stood off to the side by herself. I caught a look at her delicate profile and saw myself married to her forever, even at the advanced ages of sixty and fifty-eight and nine months. Us still together into perpetuity, like Astaire and Rogers, and Bogart and Hepburn, and Bogart and Bacall, and Nicholson and Ratchett. She looked so pretty standing there near the mustard that I couldn't stand it. "Wow," I said to myself in my mind disbelievingly.

After I bought our hot dogs (I'd forgotten about the tax, which precluded me from buying sodas), I took them over to her so we could romantically spread relish and mustard on them, but there was some guy standing with her. He had big white teeth and tanned skin and wore a blue suit. "Hi," I said with wary suspicion, handing the hot dog to Carly.

The guy with the white teeth shook my hand with great vigor. "Glad to meet you, my friend," he said televangelically.

I led Carly by the elbow back to our seats. The game introductions were starting. But after we'd sat down, I realized that in my haste to extricate us from the white-toothed blue-suited fellow, I'd forgotten about dressing our dogs. "I'm sorry," I said, with great mortification. "I don't have enough for sodas, and I've forgotten the relish. I'll be right back."

"That's all right," she said, her eyelids fluttering intermittently. "I have some." And she gave me two balled-up dollar bills.

"I'll be right back," I told her with cheerful reticence.

"All right," she said, blushing to her roots.

"W-What will it be?" said the guy behind the counter, stuttering effortlessly.

"Two small cokes," I hollered vehemently at him through the crowd noise.

On my way back to our seats, I was so hungry that I chewed gnawingly on my hot dog. But I had trouble finding my seat because I couldn't find where Carly was. Then I got an usher who looked at my ticket, brought me over to our seats—empty of Carly—and held out his palm. I thanked him effusively.

"You are welcome," he answered with a coarse gesture.

I looked all around, but Carly was nowhere. The fellows behind me were watching the game and drinking beer. A few of them looked like they knew something but wouldn't look at me.

After a few minutes of hardly watching the game, I caught a fellow in a gray suit trying to sit down in Carly's seat. "No," I said desperately, putting her soda on the seat. "It's taken."

"Doesn't look like it's taken," he replied with impeccable logic, but moved along.

I didn't watch the first half of the game but kept looking back for her. Finally one of the guys sitting behind me leaned over. "She left with some guy," he said darkly.

"Yeah, so face front, will ya?" added another guy insensitively.

I faced front, but then turned around to the first guy again.

"Did the guy have big white teeth?" I inquired, arching one eyebrow.

"I have no idea," the guy scoffed, tangling up his two.

## In Front of the Garden

I sat poutingly for the rest of the game, but at end it became very close and exciting, and even though I didn't shout with everyone else, I pumped my fist when the Knicks got to within two points with two seconds left. Patrick Ewing got to the foul line with a chance to tie the game, but he missed the first shot and then had to clang the second on purpose, and I bemoaningly groaned "darn" with everyone else when the Knicks lost.

I wandered outside and stood near a huge potted plant because I'd missed the 9:34 train and had to take the 10:16. Some guy came up to me and wanted a dollar but I told him I only had a quarter left.

"I'll take that, then," he said to me drolly, following me for a step or two.

"No, I need it," I replied alarmingly, and hurried away while his devilish laughter chased me from behind.

## The Long Ride Home

On the train I watched the dark blur outside my window until the conductor, a different guy with a maze of wrinkles on his face, asked me for my ticket. I readily proffered mine, and remembered with great relief that Carly still had hers. But then I thought of what could've happened to her, that maybe she wasn't safe, and that maybe the guy with the white teeth kidnapped her and took her off somewhere. When the conductor made his way back up the aisle after collecting tickets, I looked at him with profuse agitation, and he looked back at me with mild bewilderment as he passed. By the time the train reached Huntington, I stared wildly out the window into the darkness, positive that Carly was dead or something. Panting with great distress, I imagined the police questioning me when I got off the train.

"There was some guy with big white teeth, talking to her," I say desperately in my mind to one officer.

"A guy with white teeth, huh?" says the officer with uninhibited scorn. "Save it for the warden."

"Yeah, save it for the judge," says another officer, correcting the first.

"Right. Save it for the warden *after* you save it for the judge," says the first officer, argumentatively.

## With Doleful Vexation

### Her Parents Again

After I got off the train I ran over to Carly's costly home and rapped on the door in a panic-stricken state.

The mother answered the door this time, with her mad face, and her father was right behind with his bloated one.

"Is Carly here?" I asked them with trembling voice, looking all around.

"No," answered the mother with shrill exasperation.

"Because we were at the game, and then I went to get the relish, and when I came back with the usher she was gone," I said hastily.

"Game? What happened to the movies?" asked her mother shrewishly.

"I had tickets to the Knicks, but then she just disappeared. There was a guy—a guy with white teeth. I don't know what happened to her. Maybe we should call the police."

"Oh, my dear God," said the mother aghast, looking back at the father with wild unbelieving eyes. "Is this guy for real?"

And while she said this, she closed the door slowly in my face without looking.

### Basketball

For the first part of my walk home, I wondered which guy her mother didn't know was for real, me or the guy with the teeth. But then her words rang more sarcastically and hauntingly in my mind. Then I was mad, because maybe something really did happen to Carly, and meanwhile they were being all bloated and sarcastic about it. I tried to think about basketball instead, about that great game—except for Ewing clanging them at the end.

"I can make eighty percent of my free throws," I say ostentatiously to her parents in my mind, placing my foot in the closing door. "My record is eighty-five out of one hundred free throws," I continue sneeringly. "I'll show you who's for real."

And the rest of the way home I imagined playing them all, one against four: pointing out a blue jay and stripping the ball from Carly, then elbowing that guy in his white teeth, sending them cascading onto the court, then fouling the father hard on both arms when he attempts to shoot, and finally stuffing the mother's layup back into her contorted face and giving her a facial with a vicious and for real dunk.

Ma met me at the door upon my grand entrance, and when she questioned whether I had a good time or a bad time, I asked her if there was any food.

"Where is the pin to pump up my basketball, Ma?" I wondered later with full mouth. "Because tomorrow, Ma," I added with doleful vexation, stabbing a fresh forkful, "I'll be outside shooting baskets all day."

# THE FLY MASSACRE

Faced with another Saturday morning of waving away flies during my daughter Maggie's horse riding lesson, my six-year-old son and I thought long and hard before reaching for the fly swatters on our way out the door. He chose the yellow swatter, leaving me stuck with the pink one—although the pink had its advantages: it was stronger and easier to grip, and maybe the flies, if not color-blind, would be mesmerized by the pink long enough for me to take advantage of their hesitation and smash them.

It was all about self-defense, I explained to Stan in the car. We were simply going to swat the ones that bothered us, and leave the rest alone. But while we waited near the benches in front of the barn, they all bothered us, so Maggie grabbed the yellow swatter and went on a rampage, nailing one after another on the hot concrete ground. Luckily for the rest of them, her instructor appeared and she had to get her horse ready, so she flipped the swatter back to Stan.

At first Stan was more interested in the cat that lay in the shade. He often went along to these lessons just so he could pet one of the two cats. He was good with animals. Little chicks, dogs, turtles, rabbits. He took good care of them. He was afraid of most bugs, though.

I sat on the cast-iron bench in front of the barn, remembering my brother-in-law who once stopped me from swatting at a fly with a towel. He caught it easily with two cupped hands. "Come here, baby," he said and opened the back door to set it free.

Every living thing was precious, yes, I thought, waving a few flies away from my face but slapping at one (with lightning speed, I thought) that landed on my leg. It was long gone by the time my hand crashed into my thigh.

My son continued to pet the cat gently. We'd looked in a book about space the night before, and discovered that there were one hundred billion galaxies in space, or something like that, or maybe that our own sun was one hundred billion years old. Or both. "Amazing," I said aloud while Stan urged me to move on and read more, but I just kept saying "amazing," so he went on to other things.

Amazing—all those galaxies and suns, I thought, and we're the only ones kicking around? Maybe our souls fly off to other worlds, and then to still others, over and over again. Maybe there really can be time travel. Or maybe (I swatted at the fly on my thigh again—the same damn one, I imagined) there was nothing at all, and we just croaked into blackness, pointlessly getting older and wiser. Meaningless self-development. Nature cyclical, all about renewal, but not for us? Life beautiful, but pointless?

Can't be, I thought.

Probably is, I frowned.

Several flies were on the ground near my feet. I chose one and nailed him hard with the swatter. Found another, smashed him. Cracked another, splat. My son came over, watching me kill another, and another. Missed only one—the one that kept landing on my thigh, probably. The others either smashed flat or showed a little white underbelly-sack if they flipped over on their sides. My son flailed at a few on the ground, but they got away.

"Come at them from above," I advised him. He tried, but he came from behind one first and it darted away before he could bring the swatter high.

"You know, I think they can see behind themselves or something, but they can't see up, or they don't look up, so get close, bring it straight down, and then pop them, like this." I killed one. "And another, like this." Got one on the bench next to me. "And like that." He smashed one into the concrete, and he knew. He'd learned.

I stood up. The barn door was aluminum with little crevices. It was hard to get them when they were close to the crevices, so I waited until I had clean shots. Stan got busy at the barn's entrance, easily smashing them into the wood. We were briefly interrupted by a curious wasp, so we sat clear of it and behaved, but when the wasp drifted away we got busy again.

"I think we got at least fifty already, Stan," I said.

One of the barn workers walked by and looked over with knit brows. "We're getting rid of your fly problem," I explained to her sheepishly.

"Good luck with that," she laughed.

Stan and I switched places. I drifted quietly into the barn, careful not to scare the horses, and tap-tap-tapped at flies on the barn wall, dropping them one after another into the dirt.

"Dad, I got the green one," Stan exclaimed from outside, and I went out with him to inspect it.

"Good shot. They're fast," I said.

And we went back to work. Fly carcasses were everywhere. Was it just blackness for them, I wondered, waving one away from my face, or did they move on to fly heaven—or hell for the ones that were particularly pesky. Did they (whack!) have more chances to live, or (crack!) was this all there was for them, dying quick deaths on a horse farm? Or maybe (I hesitated) I'd be called to account, my soul stopped on its journey, a huge palm halting me. "Oh, no you don't," a Voice might say.

"What do you mean?"

"Remember the fly massacre?"

"The fly—" and then my soul realizing it had blown everything.

Stan called me to come out and watch the ants carry away dead flies. We watched a large black ant drag one of the deceased to his hidey hole. Stan raised his yellow swatter, but I stopped him. "No, that's dinner for the ants," I said. So we agreed not to kill any ants. Only (slam!) flies. One landed on my chest and I missed it entirely and wacked myself in the face. No one saw it.

Because I was slightly injured, I went after them with a vengeance, spinning and zonking a string of them splat into the wood door. "I'm getting quicker, Stan," I announced.

I went after one on the lower part of the door. He saw me coming and escaped, but in his panic he flew right into a spider web at the edge of the door. "Wow, Stan, he got stuck," I said, and we both bent to watch the fly struggle to get out. We waited for the owner of the web to crawl over and claim its meal, but after a while we figured it must have been busy somewhere else.

"You know, that's a terrible way to go," I said to my son. "Let's get him out of there." So I poked a little with the swatter until the fly was free but dazed and wiggling on the concrete ground. Whack! "That's better," I concluded.

The hour went quickly. Stan and I watched several more ants hurry away fly carcasses. Soon we were able to sit comfortably without a fly happening by. But just when we were feeling complacent, a whole new shift came buzzing around us, and we took up our swatters again. Soon the trainer came out of the barn with Maggie, breaking our concentration. "Okay, she did great," she said. My daughter was sweating fiercely. "I asked her why she wore that long sleeve shirt and she said she didn't like the flies bothering her."

"Well, we killed about two hundred or so," I said importantly, "so I don't think they'll be a problem for a while. But if any more show up, give us a call."

"I'll do that," she said, smiling crookedly.

Leaving the carnage behind, we went to the ice cream shop down the road. Stan ordered black raspberry. Maggie ordered the blueberry. And I ordered nothing, figuring I'd finish both of theirs.

"Two hundred flies," I sighed to them, but Stan was busy keeping his black raspberry from dripping, and Maggie, still sweating, was down to the cone part already. I looked out the shop window, at a little fish pond.

"Gone to the next world," I mused. Or eliminated from this beautiful one, I thought—smushed into oblivion.

# A TEEN TALE

Dear Three Editors:
I noticed from your masthead that you must be a family run rag since your names end the same way, and I'll bet that at least two of you are married to each other and the third one is your father or brother or maybe just some third wheel. I like most of your stories, except for the short ones that have no conversation or characters or plot in them. And your poems are pretty nice, except for the ones about cranberry bogs, which I must admit generally don't excite me, even when the subject comes up during my daily interactions— which is hardly ever.

This is my first teen story, as my type of writing has so far been aimed at mature literate types only, like for instance my recent story about an old woman who made it her business to free a sad-looking ape from the zoo. It is a gut-retching tale to say the least, but I'm still not finished with the end. In my first try at the story the ape escapes the grasp of the old woman and scoots away, leaving her sitting alone and learning an important lesson, which is either not to try freeing apes in the first place, or simply deciding to bring a leash next time. I'm still working on it.

Anyway, without any further to-do, here is my teen story. It is a subtle tale about the perils of teen life—which I know all about, having barely escaped mine—and I hope you like it and that your mag does leather binding.

## "A Teen Tale"

Arnold, a shy sophomore, was a real loser. Everyone hated him, even his guidance counselor; meanwhile, he was crazy for Julie, a senior cheerleader whose father drank and whose mother was having an affair with a dairy farmer. But since Julie was by far the most popular senior in the school, no one knew about her crummy home life except her best friend Suzie, whom everyone in school hated because she was the most popular girl's best friend and therefore thought she was all that.

Anyway, Julie didn't know that Arnold, the loser, was even alive. Then one night some of Julie's friends called her to go out for a ride, but her father beat her before she could get out of the house. The friends, all twelve of them, had decided to drive Suzie's mom's Toyota down Bell Hill, which had black ice all over it. Arnold the loser lived near the top of Bell Hill, and he was outside looking up at the stars when the twelve of them stopped to ask if he wanted to ride with them or go on being such a miserable dud. He almost climbed into the car, so he'd stop feeling like such a dud, but his dead grandmother whispered in his ear, "Don't be an idiot," and he backed away. All twelve joy riders gave him the finger and then tore down the hill on the black ice.

Julie limped over to the top of the hill where Arnold was, cursing a blue streak because she'd just missed the fun. But then they heard the screeching brakes and some awful laughing and screaming, followed by a series of crashes. Julie let slip a blood-curdling scream and started bawling to beat the band, but when Arnold tried to drape a comforting arm around her shoulder, she shook him off. "Get lost, creep," she said.

Later Arnold slumped at the kitchen table, cringing over the memory of Julie's angry face.

"What the hell's that?" his father asked, overhearing the many sirens.

"I don't know. A crash," Arnold answered, annoyed, moping over Julie's "get lost creep," which rang in his ears.

All twelve teens, in the hospital with concussions and broken legs and arms, had been bullies who'd picked on kids in their school, so everyone cried a blue streak over them. The teachers cried blue streaks too, but one young female teacher suffered the conniption fits of her students when she said, "Oh well," to a class, and chuckled. There was a general uproar and some gnashing of teeth that abruptly ended when the bell rang for the next class.

Meanwhile Arnold's father, who worked as a guard at Riker's Island, didn't know why his son was such a scrawny loser. "You should've been in that car—like a man," grumped his father, but Arnold's dead grandma whispered in his ear, "Don't listen to him; he's an ass."

"All right, Grandma," Arnold blurted, and his father took it to heart and beat him.

Bruised purple the next day, Arnold went to the library instead of going to math class. Miss Shrump, the teacher who'd said "Oh well," told him he looked good with his face all battered like that, and Arnold bowed his head in shame.

"You too, Julie," Arnold heard her say, and he looked over to find Julie near a stack of century-old encyclopedias. Her face was even more beaten up than his face, and so he ached for her; but when she looked over at him she mouthed two words that aren't appropriate for teen audiences but which all teens probably say to each other every day, at least once.

Still, Arnold knew that he and Julie were meant for each other because of their mutually beaten faces, so he talked to his guidance counselor and hoped that she could talk with him and Julie to-gether, but the guidance counselor told him to get the hell out of her office. All day long the guidance counselor felt bad for telling Arnold to get the hell out of her office, so she yelled at the next kid who asked for help and forgot all about feeling bad over Arnold.

More determined than ever to put an end to his anguish once and for all, Arnold walked to Julie's house after dinner that night to share his feelings with her. But her father answered, and when Arnold asked for Julie, her father said she'd run off with a carnival barker and wasn't available at the moment. Then he slammed the door in Arnold's face.

Meanwhile, Julie, eavesdropping from upstairs, heard the whole exchange and watched out her bedroom window while Arnold stood outside listening to his dead grandmother tell him not to believe the father, that he was an ass. Julie saw Arnold's bruised face in the moonlight, and was so moved by his loser-like passion, and the fact that he had no chance with her, that she began to kind of like the guy a little bit. Later, when her father asked who the loser at the door was, she screamed a blue streak at him and he thrashed her to within an inch of her life, stopping just short of killing her because he didn't want to get in trouble with the law or anything.

Julie saw Arnold at school the next day, and she tried to talk to him, but he avoided her, which was easy because she limped badly, bent way over to one side because of broken ribs, and her face was even puffier and yet more smashed in than it was before. She looked more beautiful to Arnold than ever.

Arnold felt the urge to hurt someone, or hurt himself—or better yet hurt something inanimate, if he could only get hold of an easily breakable item; but he was too much of a wuss to do anything about his sorrow. Miss Shrump saw him sulking in the hallway between classes and told him to relax, that this was only the beginning of his troubles. That cheered Arnold up. He thought of his future, of maybe becoming a forest ranger or something and disappearing into forests, and the rest of the day he wondered what forest rangers even did, so his mind was off Julie for a while.

Weeks went by. It was spring, and Arnold still wouldn't let Julie come near him, but she kept trying anyway. Soon all the unmaimed popular kids left in the school were calling Julie a loser for chasing after some stupid sophomore. She didn't care, though, and finally ran away from home after her father conked her over the head with a shovel. The same night, Arnold ran away when his father stuffed him into the clothes dryer after overhearing Arnold sigh.

"You goddamn sissy," his father seethed, slamming the dryer door closed on him. Arnold's grandmother's ghost opened the door for Arnold, though, after his father had gone upstairs to clean his Taser, and Arnold squeezed himself out just as his dad came back down the stairs.

"Thanks, Grandma," Arnold said aloud and luckily beat it out of the house before his father got to him.

So Julie and Arnold had both run away overnight and then skipped school the next day. They roamed through town, turning corners and going into and out of stores at exactly the wrong moments and just missing each other. Back at the school, some other losers had been planning to stink bomb the hallways, but they lived in the country and could only think of using cow dung. They did succeed in stinking up the place, to the student body's delight, but were later caught with some of it still on them and were arrested for assault.

Julie walked into a coffee shop in town and saw Arnold sitting at a table, preoccupied with picking lint out of his hair. She took a deep breath and sat across from him and they had breakfast together. Arnold wouldn't say much at first, but when she felt at his bruises he loosened up and felt at her bruises too. Pretty soon they were getting along okay, and she told him that even though he was a creep and a loser, she thought that maybe they could be friends.

Arnold smiled a little, and his dead grandmother whispered in his ear, "Kiss her, right now."

"No, Grandma," he said aloud.

This caused a serious misunderstanding between him and Julie for a while, but outside, after he told her all about his dead grandmother, she kind of understood. Their squabble had brought them closer, and much to their mutual relief, and mindful of their bruises, they gingerly kissed a blue streak.

# THE WRONG BETH

Back in my late high school days, Beth Carson sat high on the open stairs eating an apple on the art department side of the school. I stopped below and looked up at her pretty, easy-going self. "Is...that apple green?" I stammered.

Her mouth opened a little and she looked down at me. "What?"

"I mean, is it...good?" She nodded yes, that it was good, and yes to the greenness of it, maybe, but I had nothing else to say beyond that and drifted away. On the way to gym class I called myself a simpleton and would have bopped myself in the nose if I'd had the nerve.

The same day, or maybe it was the next day after a class, I staggered towards the smell of cafeteria food when Candace Something came out of nowhere and gave me a folded paper with "From Beth" written on it. I stopped in the middle of the hallway and opened it, wondering briefly if it was about the apple. But it was a poem. I scanned through words written in a heavy, scraggly hand—words like "love" and "sky," and one "tree," and a "dachshund" for some reason, and then down at the bottom I saw the name, "Beth Birdsell." I folded the paper and groaned inside, remembering the thick dark eyebrows and the overeager laugh of the Beth from theater class. What the hell. Beth Birdsell? I frowned, and the next moment caught her dark eyes, sad under thick eyebrows, as she crossed the hall at a distance and hung her head. From the cafeteria door I scowled after her as if to say, "Why this Beth?"

In the cafeteria line I remembered my idiotic, "Is that apple green?" to the real Beth, my Beth, and I shoved the poem deep into my front pocket. Later, I glowered out of the cafeteria window at a science project garden, chewing slowly on my hamburger while the image of the wrong Beth's sad eyes punished me.

Afternoon classes stunk, as usual, except for the very last one, *Values*, which had only six of us. We got into a discussion about *Little House on the Prairie* (I brought it up), but I couldn't say what I wanted to say about it because I got into a laughing fit when I tried to talk. It was funny to me because life in their world was so simple and perfect—the Reverend talking to the town and everyone crying at the drop of a hat and the music getting all swollen—but I couldn't say any of that because I cracked up every time I started. Soon all of us were laughing, including Dr. Silver. He dabbed at his eyes, finally getting enough breath to say that he hadn't laughed so hard in years. It was the funniest five minutes of the day, and none of us knew why we were laughing.

So that cheered me up a little.

The bus ride home cheered me up too. I always sat up front with Marjorie Adams, and we usually talked easily and laughed about nothing. That day, it was about the lady bus driver's manly arms and our bet that there was either a tattoo of a tick or a birthmark on her forearm. We pointed and guessed.

This bus driver often drove pretty fast, but now she tore out wildly, speeding over the tracks and along Edgewood Road, scaring us all to death, especially Marjorie and me—first to fly headlong out the window if we crashed. We wondered if she'd heard us laughing about her tattoo (or birthmark, Marjorie still insisted over the engine's roar).

# The Wrong Beth

In between our gasps of terror, at a red light, I told Marjorie about the two Beths, about the green apple, and the poem, and the wrong Beth's ghastly look—everything. Marjorie called me an idiot. The wrong Beth was nice, she said, just sensitive was all. And she didn't know Beth Carson, except that she seemed a bit snooty. I shook my head as the light turned green, and I had just enough time to wonder aloud why the heck things couldn't just be *simple* before the driver made us all slam over to the right (me into the window) with a deadly forty mph turn onto Third Avenue.

During college spring break four years later, I took my daily walk to the harbor, holding Heidegger's *Being and Time,* required reading for my Existentialism class. Heidegger and that professor and all my genius classmates had meant to tell me that life was incomprehensible, that whatever I thought was real wasn't really real or something, and so I only flipped through the book, slowing down along Third Avenue to gape at words like "phenomenological" and "temporal" and "being." I saw quite a few words like "were" and "the" and "from" as well, but they were no help. I was tempted to backtrack home and grab the Lao Tzu book from my Confucianism and Taoism class instead. That was understandable philosophy, at least: the weakest things in the world overcome the strongest; water wears away rock. Instead, I walked on toward the harbor, using Heidegger for alternating biceps curls.

A white Volkswagen with its top down stopped ahead of me near the church, slanted my way so that I could see a girl leaning over the passenger seat, her wind-blown hair half in her face. "You want a ride? Where are you heading?"

I hesitated. "The harbor. But maybe just to the library." She waved me in.

"How have you *been*?" she asked me, and peeled out along Third Avenue. She smiled and her hair blew everywhere.

"Pretty good."

"I'm doing all right too. Going to Stony Brook now. I'm on break."

"Me too. Stony Brook too." I had to clear my throat. "Break too."

"Neat." She laughed. "I can bring you all the way to the harbor, but I have to stop at home first. I forgot something."

"Oh, don't bother. Anywhere is all right. Library's good."

"No bother. Just take a second." She laughed again. "My mother keeps telling me, she tells me I would forget my own head—" She passed a left-turning truck and barreled blindly across the busy intersection, and I pushed backward as though slamming on brakes. "I'd forget my own head if it wasn't attached."

The wind had blown her hair clear of her dark eyebrows, and wide-eyed, I looked from her to the trees flying by on the passenger side. I remembered her crestfallen face in the hallway four years before, but now she returned my terrified look with a cheerful one.

"I drive too fast?"

"No, no, it's okay. But do you have any seatbelts around?" I felt under me.

"No, my father buried them way under the seats. He said it was more dangerous wearing them." She made a sharp turn down a side street, parallel with the high school. "I'll be quick, though, don't worry." She cut up to Edgewood, made a left past the high school, and turned onto a narrow side road. The Volkswagen's engine in back roared and popped, and I felt myself inwardly trying to climb in a spiral to the trees above. She turned hard again. Foliage flew past.

"Isn't this a one way road?" I shouted through the din.

She smiled wide under her flying hair. "No." And she thundered up another narrow tree-lined road. "Almost there," she screamed, and floored it.

I twisted in my seat, my words stuck in my throat mid-gasp. She turned so suddenly up a stone driveway that I almost fell into her lap, and then she braked hard in front of a two-story house. Everything quiet now, she bit at her lower lip and exhaled. "Whew."

I stared at the lip. "I think we need to take the seatbelts out."

She snorted a laugh. "I'll be right back." And she burst out of the car, running to the house and up a set of wood steps to the second floor.

I dug under me for seat belts and looked all around—at the woods-enclosed property, up to the second floor of the house, and then out to the road. My hand clenched the door handle from the eighth to the tenth minute of waiting, before finally pulling it. I hurried down the driveway to the street.

"What a nut," I laughed, walking downhill, but when I heard a roaring engine behind me around a blind turn, I jumped down into the woods, my jeans, bare arm, and Heidegger's front cover catching nothing but mud as I slid down. A small pick-up truck went by.

For twenty minutes I stood, listening and wiping mud off my book, jeans and arm. Two cars passed but no white Volkswagen, so I climbed up onto the road, walking fast at first, and then running, having no idea to where. I'd seen *Papillion* once, and for a while I was Papillion—hurrying away, with no wasted motion, expecting darts blown at me from all sides and me leaping in slow motion off a hill.

Finally, I reached the end of the road and saw Route 25A to the right. It would lead to Church Street and then to Main Street, at the end of which was the harbor, and I breathed easier, walking unafraid along sidewalks like a civilized person again.

Soon the diner and the ice cream shop, the docks, and the water were all ahead of me on Main Street, and I wiped the back of my still-muddy hand across my forehead. "What a crazy-person."

A little later, after coffee and toast at the diner, I came out to find the white Volkswagen parked directly across the street in front of the hardware store. It wasn't even running, and it looked sinister just sitting there. I headed down Main Street toward the park—no sign of her anywhere—and wound up at the band shell, where I could see her car and wait for her to leave (or run if she spotted me and tried to chase me down or smash me flat in the middle of the park lawn or against the band shell).

Near the end of my hour-long vigil under the band shell, I imagined her upstairs in her house, maybe having peeked with one eye out a window corner, laughing at me when I'd scrambled out of the car. But then again, I thought (looking across the park at the seagulls and the docked boats bobbing in the water), she had been friendly, and there was no meanness in her eyes, just some kind of certifiably insane love of life. She loved dachshunds, after all, and so I imagined her instead coming out of the house (after having gone to the bathroom or changing clothes or finally finding some lost thing) and shrugging or shaking her head or frowning deeply at the sight of her empty car.

I could hear my old bus buddy Marjorie chuckle and call me an idiot either way.

She appeared at last, hurrying along the sidewalk toward her car, her dark hair still flying in front of her face, and she threw a flat bag into the back seat. I crept out from under the band shell as she started the Volkswagen. She backed up the wrong way against the slant of parked cars, and raced up South Street, past the playground and the basketball courts and up the hill.

Like some fugitive I crossed the park, and didn't even consider taking her South Street shortcut to the library, certain of my Main Street and Laurel Avenue path. No crazy, winding, back road shortcuts for me: life simple and straight—the Lao Tzu way.

I winced...and tossed muddy Heiddeger into the corner trash.

# THE SPY AND THE PRIEST

There was no way the Russians were ever going to overcome the world unless they could overcome the United States. That was the firm conviction of all the Russian officials who gathered in the Very Important Room for tea and some Russian food which the author cannot spell, when—after Brezhnev, the clown of the bunch, amused them all by impersonating Ronald Reagan with a Russian lisp—they all sat down to the most dire business at hand: no, not which cakes to have at the next meeting, but the way to conquer the United States!

It was the very gruff Ivan Spatulishnotskutchkinitski who cleared his throat after the others had finally stopped drying their eyes and after a final whoop of laughter burst from them when Brezhnev accidentally sat in the strawberry crepe suzette.

"I thought this meeting was going to be important," Ivan said. "For need I remind you, because we are in the Very Important Room, very important things must be discussed. If not, if we fail to arrive at one very important decision or discuss one very important subject—and *not* like last time, how the Mets will do this year— then we are in violation of the Kremlin."

"Okay then, Ivan, you party pooper," yawned Dmitry, Brezhnev's right hand man, "what's important that can be discussed?"

"The United States."

"That was last time," Dmitry said, snorting.

"That was the Mets!" Ivan screamed, pounding his fist on the Very Important Table. Everyone was silent; there was not one sound. All that could be heard, while they all looked, amazed, at Ivan's red face, was the faint whistling sound of Brezhnev's nose as he inhaled.

"Now, I have a daring proposition for you," Ivan began. "If you will buy it—uh, I mean, agree on it—we can conquer the world. It came to me while I was getting ready for bed last night. I took off my pants; then I put them on again. Then, realizing my absence of mind, I took them off once more. Then again I put them on un- thinkingly. I did this *eleven* times before finally going to bed with them on, too exhausted to try again. I said to myself, 'We are a weak people, we Russians. Oh, we can blow the world to smithereens without having to tip our hats, but so what—the United States can do the same without tipping theirs.' I speak figuratively, of course, for those of you I see trying to figure that out. There is one thing standing in our way, though. We cannot beat the United States be- cause they have God and we only have the government. Oh, the government is a wondrous thing, I beg of you, Mr. Brezhnev, better, even better than God, of course, in a practical, efficient way, but (he cleared his throat loudly) not when it comes to rolling in the bucks, not when it comes to popularity and glory. We always see it in the movies, how God is for the good old United States. They have all the religious leaders on their side and the Pope on their side. If we can understand why God likes them so much, if we can understand what makes God tick, if we can find out what gets His goat and where His weakness is, we can beat Him. Once we knock off God, we can conquer the world!"

"Very interesting, Ivan," Brezhnev said after a long pause. "But you know I get big headaches when I think of God."

158

"You don't have to," Ivan said. His eyes were blazing now. He gestured to the door and a man appeared from out of the shadows, a slight man with greasy hair and bushy eyebrows and big eyes. "This is a spy," Ivan said. "And he is going to find out about God for us."

All of the men stopped chewing their cakes simultaneously and turned their eyes on the spy, who bowed extremely low in slow motion. "Gentlemen," he said.

His name was Yoramin Rhezvinski, and he had been a spy since the age of six—not a professional spy, mind you, just a household one as a youngster. Such were his talents at such an early age, however, that he drove his family half-mad. As soon as he could write he was filling memo pads with the details of the events in his household and sending them to the Kremlin. Fortunately for Yoramin's father, who described himself as being at his wit's end every moment since Yoramin's birth, the evidence against his family was not substantial. For instance, Yoramin noted that his father wore a moose head to bed. This did not draw attention from the government, although some members, including Brezhnev himself, wore a moose head to bed in anticipation of its benefits. There were none. Instead, when Brezhnev awoke the next morning, he thought he was a moose, and as he looked at himself in the mirror, he said, "At least it's not hunting season. What a target I would make in the middle of Moscow," before realizing what was really going on.

Yoramin became an exchange student and went to school in the United States for a year before returning with a sack of notebooks filled with his observations, complete conversations with professors and students, and some jokes and riddles he'd heard. He sent these notebooks to Brezhnev, but Leonid, remembering his moose head scare, sent the notebooks back with a harsh warning not to send him anything again.

This discouraged Yoramin greatly, and he walked the streets of Moscow, depressed. He had taken up with his parents again, but spent as little time as possible with them. Though despondent about his apparent failure as a spy, he would not give up and sent his notes to various government officials in the hope of getting noticed. They always wound up in the hands of Brezhnev again, and Brezhnev sent them back with a stricter warning each time.

Finally, Ivan Spatulishnotskutchkinitski turned up at Yoramin's door one evening and described his scheme for defeating the United States through finding out about God and destroying Him.

"I'm a spy," Yoramin declared, "not an evangelist."

"All you have to do is inform us about what you find out. I have seen your work. You are very detailed and observant, and your jokes and riddles are excellent, but I saw nothing about God. I know He goes over big over there, so I want you to go back there, as a student again, and do your spying thing. I want the whole poop. Now...I've made all the arrangements. All we have to do is convince Brezhnev."

"*You* convince him. He'll kill me."

"Don't worry about the moose head incident. We'll give you a fake name. How about Nikolai Ivanovich? He's never seen you."

"Do you know what you're saying?" Yoramin said, aghast.

"No," Ivan retorted.

"If they find out, we're both dead men. They have records and photos..."

"Big deal. You naïve little spy. Brezhnev will never double check me. Me? Ivan Spatulishnotskutchkinitski? Now, let's go. To the Kremlin, and then...the United States of America!" Ivan laughed explosively, like a demon, his eyes wild, triumphant.

"Just a minute. Could I finish my blintz first?" Yoramin asked.

Before we learn of Yoramin's adventures in the United States, let us have a look at poor Ivan Spatulishnotskutchkiniski's fate.

After having successfully convinced Brezhnev, and while Yoramin was on his way to the United States, Ivan enjoyed dinner over at Brezhnev's Eating Room. He sat back in his chair and belched. Brezhnev, sitting beside him, belched too, and both men seemed to be admiring each other's belching abilities. In between belches, however, Leonid surveyed Ivan carefully. He mused silently for twenty minutes or so before he spoke:

"That spy you introduced seems awfully familiar."

Ivan laughed loudly. "He is just your average run of the mill spy. He will succeed in his mission, though, I assure you, Leo. May I call you Leo?"

Brezhnev growled.

"I mean, he is a great spy, Mr. Leo—Mr. Brezhnev," Ivan stammered.

Brezhnev nodded, sinking his chin into his fist and staring into Ivan's eyes. Ivan belched again, but Brezhnev did not stir. Soon Ivan began sweating profusely as Brezhnev moved his eyes to within two inches of Ivan's eyes and spoke slowly.

"When you introduced this spy before, I noticed something very familiar about his manner and his language. With everything he said, he seemed to have the idea that he wanted to prove himself as a spy. And when I mentioned the incident from long ago, when an impudent little weasel kid drove my colleagues half-mad with that moose head report, his choking fit was very suspicious to me." Ivan had loosened his collar was looking at the ceiling and whistling to himself.

"As though he was not who you said he was," Brezhnev added, with emphasis.

Ivan fell at Brezhnev's feet. "Please, Leo! All I wanted to do was save the country. Nay, cause its triumph. I knew you wouldn't approve of him, but he's the best spy I've ever come across. I had to do it!"

"You are a stupid man, Ivan. Why did you confess? You could have simply said, 'I didn't know who he was. He came to me and gave me the name Nikolai Ivanovich. How was I to know?'"

Ivan looked up. "That's right. What a blockhead I am. Then how about I say that? I didn't know who he was. He just came to me—"

Brezhnev waved his hand, shaking his head. "It's too late, Ivan."

Ivan's fate was clear, but for Yoramin, Fate was floating over and about his Being, calling itself Destiny and beckoning him to follow. So he followed what he thought was his Destiny to the United States, to New York, but he got on the wrong plane and landed in Chicago. When he finally reached New York City by train the next morning, leaving his Destiny behind to catch another train, he was determined to begin his mission immediately. After buying a tea with lemon, he surveyed the sky, but found it looked no different from the sky in Russia. How else could he tell if God liked this better than his own country? He was stumped and considered giving up. "Me? A spy of the first degree, stumped?" he cried to himself. He wanted to dash his brains out on the sidewalk. But first he paced up and down the same city block for an hour, thinking. He needed a place to stay, to sleep and eat and think and hide if necessary, and the city was no place to stay for sure. So he went to Long Island by train and slept in garbage cans for a couple of nights before he came upon a church, a large majestic building of white stone. Boy, whoever lives here must be loaded, he thought. He knocked on the door of a building branched off from the church, and soon a man answered. He wore a black shirt with a piece of white towel paper folded and taped around his neck half-way up. He greeted Yoramin with a disarming smile. "Hello, I am Father Don Rickles," he said.

"And I am Yora—I am Sam Jones," Yoramin declared.

"May I help you?"

"I am poor and broken-hearted and need a place to sleep."

"Why don't you try the Salvation Army? What does this place look like, a hotel? Just kidding. Come on in."

Yoramin (disgusted, then put off, then frightened, then pleased) entered and found himself in a small office with a white marble floor.

"I have been sleeping in garbage cans. I have eaten nothing since coming from Rus—from uh, the city."

"I see. Well, this is your home for as long as you wish. I need someone to talk to since Father Spuds Devlin left here for another parish."

Father Don Rickles led Yoramin through a hallway into a large bedroom. "I can never understand how people can leave places so easily, how they can change from one part of their lives to another and not be saddened over it."

"Unless there's a woman that causes it," Yoramin muttered to the priest bitterly.

"You mean the leaving?"

"Yes. I left my home because of a woman. Dark hair, dark eyes, a cute little mole on her cheek, a wonderful lisp. Five feet of sweetness, my sweet Katerina. I miss her. And she was going to marry me, but she married another man. A mouse of a man with an annoying mustache that I wanted to pull from both sides with all my might! He had a good job and a lot of money, so she married him. I had nothing, but she loved me! Me, do you hear! And so I left because I could no longer stand the sight of her, or even of the same trees I saw every day while I foolishly believed she would marry me."

"I see."

"I hate her and all women, the liars. I want to catapult them all into the sea. All of them!"

"Sam, no."

"Katerina first, and may she go the farthest and cause the biggest splash."

"Not at five feet she won't."

"I'll *make* her splash the most."

"You are too controlling, too bitter..."

"Oh, you are right." Yoramin patted Father Don Rickles weakly on the shoulder. "You are right, my good father. I'm really despicable, am I not? I loathe myself for thinking this way. She is the sweetest woman on earth and I love her. I want to bash my own brains out with a club!"

"Oh no, don't do—"

"But I won't because I love life too much. I love it so much that I am always holding back tears of joy. The simplest things make me go to pieces. A leaf on a tree. Two sweet potatoes. A tick."

"I don't underst—"

"Oh, I don't know how to explain. How can I tell you what's in my broken heart? It would take ten years not counting meals to explain. I want to just pluck my eyes out!"

"No, no."

"I want to smash my head into a wall. I want to pull a dumpster on top of myself. I want to *extract...each toenail* from my left foot one at a time in slow motion."

"Enough," Father Don Rickles said firmly, switching the lights of the room off and on, off and on.

"But you don't understand. I just want to die."

"Die? Don't say that. That's all I need. Every day another funeral; each day another old man or woman dies with the histories of their lives still on their failing lips. I am tired of death. If I knew I was going to be around it so much I would have become a doctor, or a cook."

"Well," Yoramin started to say, but an alarm clock rang loud and insistently from inside another room.

"I am sorry but it is my bedtime," Father Don Rickles explained. "We will talk more in the morning. I can tell we have much to discuss and many things to share." Yoramin nodded vigorously. "Good night, then, Mr. Jones, until tomorrow."

Father Don Rickles left and Yoramin paced the room, confused that the priest hadn't offered him any food. Here it was, only eight o'clock, and all the lights were turned off and the priest was already snoring in the next room. Yoramin got under the covers of his bed and soon felt himself becoming sleepy.

"I almost believed some of the things I was saying," he chuckled to himself. "In any case, it's working. Wait, what's working?" He sat up, terrified, not knowing who he was. At last he remembered that he was a spy and settled down to rest. Before he slept, though, he snapped his fingers and cursed himself in a low voice. "Forgot to ask him about God. Must remember to in the morning."

Yoramin jolted awake at noon to the most God-awful rendition of "Somebody Loves Me" that he'd ever heard. He followed the voice to the other side of the building where he spotted Father Don Rickles near some hedges with a disheveled man whose horse-like teeth flared while he sang. Yoramin watched in horror as the man boomed out the end of the song, holding the final "...maybe it's you-u-u-u" for more than twenty excruciating seconds. The priest, spotting Yoramin at last, smiled and waved him over.

"Did you have a nice sleep?" asked the priest. "This is Bruce. Bruce, this is Sam."

Bruce belched, barely acknowledging Yoramin, and wandered away before turning. "I'll fix your gutters today, Father. That's a promise."

"Thank you, son."

Yoramin glared after Bruce, who slouched away. "What a lousy singer. He's not going to fix any gutters."

"He is one of God's children. I think I can help him. He fixed a crack in my sidewalk a year ago and has been staying here ever since. We're both Mets fans, you see—"

"The Mets are very important," said Yoramin with conviction.

"Uh—yes, yes, of course they're important," the priest conceded. "But the scriptures above all, you know." He trailed off.

"It seems as though you have your doubts," observed Yoramin as they began to walk.

"What do you mean? I have no doubts. Doubts about what?"

"It's just that it seemed to me just now that you were trying to convince yourself that the scriptures were more important than the Mets—or to baseball in general, let us say."

"That's absurd, Sam," scoffed the priest, picking frantically at freckle on his hand.

"Well, let us say that the Mets make the World Series—which is laughable with the state their pitching is in at the moment—but let us say this is true. Would you say that someone coming to your church is going to think more about the scriptures than he will about the pitching matchups?"

"He can think about both," the priest asserted wisely.

"Yes, but what I'm saying is that people don't really care about God the way they used to. Well, I don't mean *care about*. I'm sure people don't worry about God catching a cold, for instance."

"They should."

"Yes, but I mean that people aren't as *afraid* of God as they used to be."

Father Don Rickles stopped walking abruptly and clenched his fist. "That is certainly *not* so! They *better* be afraid, or God will come down on them with every inch of fury He can muster and—" The priest bit down on his lower lip, clenching both fists and falling to his knees. "Or else He'll punish them. He'll punish them for sure!" He pounded the walkway with his bare fists.

From the side of the church Bruce let go of the ladder and started toward them, but the priest looked up suddenly and held up his hand. "I'm all right, Bruce," he said, and Bruce stepped uncertainly back to the ladder.

Yoramin was completely taken aback and gently took the priest by the elbow, helping him up. He could not believe that he'd seen such fury in this gentle man's face and decided not to provoke him any further. "I would just like to hear more of what you have to say about God," Yoramin whispered in a gentle voice. Bruce stepped off the ladder and began walking over again, but this time Yoramin waved him away violently with two hands and Bruce went back to the ladder.

The two men sat in the kitchen over tea. The priest seemed to have calmed himself. "Never mind about that outburst before," he said. "I would really rather hear you tell me about your life. What do you believe is important in this life?"

"I don't believe anything is important," Yoramin replied. "I have gone through twenty-five years of life, a drop in the bucket for you, maybe, but for me it is enough to realize that nothing has meaning. Love is an empty word. To love a woman is impossible. They are terrible. Men are terrible. We are all terrible, filled with such ugliness and nameless fears. Yes, love is impossible."

"What about love between brothers?" the priest asked.

"Big deal, brothers." Yoramin scoffed. Once again he'd forgotten that he was a spy on a mission, and he spilled out all that was in his heart. "It all means nothing. We will die whether we love or don't love, and loving causes pain, even if we love but mere brothers. Life is meaningless, I tell you."

"Why is it meaningless? Why is love impossible? Is it that woman again, that Katerina woman?"

"Don't even say her name."

"There are plenty of fish in the—"

"I don't want to hear that fish talk! How would you know anything at all, priest? Have you ever loved a woman, only to have her change her mind like the wind changes?"

"Well, no, but—"

"I have. It was nothing but a joke to her. Taking advantage of my sensitivity, she did. Playing games with me, like I was a worm." Yoramin buried his head in his hands and wailed. Sighing, Father Don Rickles took him gently by the elbow and led him to his room where he collapsed, weeping on his bed. Bruce put the ladder down and headed toward the building, but the priest waved him back. "It's all right, Bruce. It's him this time."

Yoramin cried for four days and four nights and hardly ate or slept. When the priest walked into the room on the fourth evening, his shoes squished on Yoramin's tears which covered the floor. He went to Yoramin's bed and addressed him in a soft voice.

"Why are you crying so much over one woman?"

Yoramin stared vacantly at the ceiling. "She wasn't just one woman."

"Well now, how is that possible?"

"It isn't just her, though. It is all of life. It bleeds suffering all around. The very air is filled with sweetness, and it is this which makes life painful. All of this sweetness is within us, the beauty, the music, Time's passing and the changing of the seasons. The snow. A fly. But it is all outside, and nothing enters. The beauty is there and I am here and nothing enters. So I am full of hatred for life...I am really a spy, you know. I may as well tell you. I came to find out about God for the Russian government, but I have already failed in my mission. They can shoot me if they want to. I can't tell them about God because even you don't know anything about Him except (mimicking) 'the scriptures, the scriptures.' I'd say to them that

God lets us suffer and for what? Heaven? We will go to Heaven if we believe, and we won't go if we don't believe? Is that some kind of game? Tell me."

The priest sighed and looked out the window at the darkness.

"Father, you know it, don't you? There's no point to life. Tell God to strike me dead. Please tell Him, Father. Go to a quiet place and ask Him to please strike me dead. He'll listen to you."

"I am totally at a loss for words, Sam," said Father Don Rickles slowly. "You are a very bitter man. You are more pathetic than even poor Bruce. He lives in a world where life is all about fixing a gutter and singing a standard. But it's better than your world. You're all clouded up with anger and I am getting very bad vibes right now, man."

At this moment Yoramin burst out furiously in another fit of tears, and Father Don Rickles drifted away from him and closed the door.

The next morning Yoramin woke to find Bruce sitting on his bed trying to feed him a muffin. Instinctively Yoramin knocked the muffin out of Bruce's hands and bolted to his feet. The priest entered and picked up the muffin as Bruce shuffled out.

"I'll fix your gutters today, Father."

"Thank you, Bruce." The priest sighed and wandered toward the kitchen, biting into the muffin. Yoramin followed. "However badly you feel, you should not treat Bruce that way, Sam."

"Because God says I should love my brothers, I suppose," said Yoramin. "And don't call me Sam. My name is Yoramin Rhezvinski. And if you know what's good for you, you won't ask me any questions about why I'm here."

"You already told me."

"Huh?"

"You told me just last night that you are a spy."

"Oh. Right. Well, then don't ask me any *more* questions, man of the cloth. I'm staying right here, and if you give me an argument I'll knock you in your nose. I may have been crying like a baby for four days and four nights, but I can be tough."

The priest whirled and socked Yoramin in the jaw, sending him sprawling onto the floor and causing three of this teeth to fly out of his mouth and cascade ahead of him along the ceramic tile.

"I can be tough, too," said the priest.

For four more days and four more nights, Yoramin healed his sore jaw and damaged gums by talking only sparingly and eating apple sauce. His mood, however, became increasingly more cheerful, his melancholy melting along with his black and blue face. He and the priest rarely spoke, but if either seemed to be angry at all it was the priest, who was not so much angry with Yoramin as he was silently brooding about other matters. Yoramin's words to him had indeed hit home somehow. He wondered what he was doing being a representative of God when he wasn't even sure what God really was. He knew that God was Something. It was the What that had him stumped. During a confession one day, a man murmured his sins through the curtain which separated him from God's ears, the priest.

"I thought of committing adultery fifteen times this week, Father. Only once did I follow through, though. Also, I haven't given back the hoe I borrowed from Sam Blake, even though he never gives my stuff back to me when he borrows. I slapped my wife around one time this week because she didn't have the ketchup on the table. And—"

"Are you finished?" the priest asked.

"No, what do you mean?"

"I mean, just go. You can say some prayers if you like, but they're useless. They're nice strong words and it all might make you feel a little better, but it won't take away what you've done no matter how many times you say the words, or in whatever devout voice you whisper them. Go read a sports section."

"Now just a second. I came here to be forgiven, not—"

"*You* wait a minute, buddy boy—"

"You're no priest. I'm leaving." He burst out of the confessional and stormed past the other sinners who were waiting on line. The priest cracked open his confessional door and roared, "Go on then! Go! Adulterer! Wife beater! Go on! And I'm going to tell Sam Blake about that hoe!"

One might say that the priest was fed up, but he wasn't completely fed up. He had his doubts about God, but more doubts about man himself. He felt that as long as he doubted he could not go on talking about Him to those who had more faith the he did. He wasn't sure why he'd ever become a priest in the first place. His brother was a bank robber and his sister a hooker, and though that makes for a good start in the forgiveness department, he wondered why he was different. His family was Catholic, so Catholic that they trimmed their bushes into the shape of the Virgin Mary each spring, so much so that they said a full rosary every night before eating dinner while their food grew cold and Don's stomach rumbled. And after an entire childhood of cold and sometimes spoiled food, his sister became anorexic and his brother became a glutton, stealing money and then buying and eating large quantities of chocolate layer and cheese cakes, so that he was exactly three hundred pounds by his fifteenth birthday. His poor family said even more rosaries for him, but his weight and his thievery only increased. Soon he became too heavy to run from the police anymore, even in sneakers, and he was caught sometimes before reaching the door of the store he was robbing even though the police station was a full three miles away.

As for his sister the whore (as he became accustomed to calling her during one of his many long and forlorn walks while mulling over his troubles), in a family with parents who considered communication as secondary to (well, they never mentioned what it might be secondary to), and in whose home there seemed to be more silence than if they were all buried six feet beneath the earth, who went along their twenty-odd years together in stiffly grim and mute conduct with each other, where everything concerning feeling was to be submerged, and learned, it seemed, by osmosis, or perhaps, on understandably emotional occasions, by the twitching of an eyebrow, she became immersed in her own world of feeling.

One spring Sunday morning when she was ten years old, as she and her parents walked to their car after church, she announced that she wanted to go to hell, saying in a playful but still serious way that hell was the place for her. After beating her, her parents explained that she wouldn't go to hell because she was a nice girl and that only bad people went to hell. "I want to be bad, though," she'd said, and from then on was determined to have her way. She started to steal like her brother, but he called her a copycat so she stopped. So then, since sex seemed like the worst sin for a Catholic until marriage, when it becomes a pardonable crime, she tried to become a tramp, first looking the word up in the college dictionary, then asking her classmates what tramps acted like, and then trying to look like one and walk like one and talk like one, so that by the time she was a teenager she was proudly announcing to her classmates, "I'm a whore," and set out to prove it to boys whom she figured wanted to be bad like her, and therefore it was better to know them now anyway so she wouldn't be seeing strangers in hell—wouldn't have to go through all the trouble of introducing herself when she first got there and all.

Young Don wanted to be a comedian, but when he realized that he wasn't funny at all, after he couldn't make a bunch of very drunk friends even smirk at any of his jokes, he decided it would be best to be named after his favorite comedian, at least. So he changed his name from Riccio to Rickles, thus also disassociating himself further from his thieving, whoring, silent family. He didn't know what to do with his life as he reached adulthood. He was shy with women, couldn't make anyone laugh, was a C average student, had no skill with his hands, and had a slight facial tic, so one day he decided that, what the hell, he would be a priest. The hours were good, and he would get to read all he wanted. Besides, it was a good way to get away from his silent family.

Now, twenty years later, he was ready to quit, long tired of his priestly life. Besides, he'd found out early on that he liked women a lot more than reading anyway. He often changed clothes and hopped into his car or on a train, traveling hundreds of miles just to allow himself a glance at a woman. Even then, sometimes he would be recognized. "Hey Father, how you doin'!" a drunk man yelled to him on a New York City subway train after he'd sat next to and said hello to a pretty blonde woman.

So, rather than go on pretending and feeling humiliated (even the memory of the drunk man's words made him shudder now), he decided to quit the priesthood. He would have to wait for Bruce to finish the gutters and put the ladder away, and for Yoramin to heal his jaw and get out, but he was determined to leave his old life behind.

A few days later, a pre-occupied Don took a morning stroll with Bruce along the garden. Bruce had begun singing "I Wish I Knew" as they passed through a white trellis when a flash of light and an audible pop made them stop. They were startled to see an angry face hovering over the ivy with liquid-like undulation. "My God," exclaimed Don, and Bruce promptly ran away, yelling something about fixing the gutters.

"Are you my cousin Roy?" Don said to the face. "Are you Roy? Roy, is that you?"

"No, it is not your cousin *Roy*," said the face. "Who's *Roy*? I am Ivan Spatulishnotskutchkinitski. Actually, his ghost."

"Ivan who?"

The face sighed. "It's not my real name. It was the name of a Russian comedian. Never mind. I don't have much time. I am looking for Yoramin Rhezvinski."

"I am taking care of him. His jaw is almost healed. What is it you want?"

"If you'll be quiet I'll tell you. I don't care about his *jaw*. Who cares about his jaw?"

The face of Ivan's ghost hovered silently for quite some time. It sank slowly until it reached a rose bush and sprang up when it settled on one of the thorns.

"Well, what is it then?" Don Rickles demanded at last.

"Oh. I've...uh, forgotten," said the ghost shamefully.

"Well, maybe if you talk around it you'll remember," suggested Don.

"Yes, good idea. But...talk around what?"

"Talk about what you've forgotten."

"I've forgotten what I've forgotten."

"You told me you were looking for Yoramin Rhez—"

"Oh yes. Right. Well, I do know that I was killed because of him. Because, you see, I'm dead. And I'll bet you can't guess how I died."

"I really don't know."

"You must guess!" the ghost of Ivan boomed.

"I don't know. Blown up?"

"Wrong! I was shot. Shot by Brezhnev himself because I sent Yoramin here to the United States against his wishes."

"Yes, I already know that Yoramin is a spy. And the Russians must be sending another spy after him, is that it?"

174

The ghost face of Ivan sank onto one of the rose bushes again and remained on a thorn. "Then I've come here for nothing," he cried out mournfully. "I get one trip a year and I used it up."

"No, yours was a very noble act, to come all this way to help a fellow spy."

"Thanks," Ivan's ghost face said brusquely, rising. "I'd better go."

"Wait!" Don called. "Could you just tell me—"

"I know, I know. What's it like? They all ask that. Don't you know that I can't tell you, silly? Just be a good person, dammit, and live well. Do your best and you will see. Yes," the ghost mused, fading, "you shall see... (fading more) buddy...boy...." The face of Ivan rose slowly, bounced suddenly off the pavement, and then shot up and disappeared into the sky.

"Amazing," Don exclaimed, already running. He ran past Bruce, who was climbing a ladder, and into the rectory.

Later, while they sat in the kitchen and drank tea, Father Don Rickles told Yoramin what he'd seen, and Yoramin wept unashamedly at the news of Ivan's death before realizing that he did not really like the man and thought he was a lunatic.

"Yes, he was crazy, but he gave me my answer. I am quitting the priesthood," said Don. "And, since they are sending someone to kill you, perhaps you would like to come with me."

"You invite me even after the way I've behaved?"

"Yes, we are friends."

"I am thunderstruck."

"Then it's decided. Get your things."

"I have no things."

"Then I'll get mine."


Father Don Rickles packed and changed his clothes. Looking into the mirror, he emphatically ripped the collar from his neck and threw it to the floor as Yoramin walked into the room.

"Are you sure this is what you want to do?" he asked Don.

"I am very sure. I am sad, but that only means a change is passing through me. It's the good kind of sadness."

"I never had the good kind of sadness, but I'm glad you're sad and that's it's the good kind. I am sad, too. But I have the bad kind of sadness."

"But you're changing. Change is good."

"You're right, if it's the good kind of change and not the bad kind of change. I was just a stupid spy before. But now the heck with spy work, the heck with my government. The heck with any government."

Suddenly a voice boomed out from across the room. "Ah ha! Got you, you weasel!" There came the trampling of the voice's owner struggling with coats and tripping over shoes in the priest's closet before a man came tumbling out head first onto the floor. He sprang up, holding a tape recorder in one hand. "I've got your confession right here," the man said to Yoramin.

"Do you need it?" Yoramin said in a steady voice. "Won't you just kill me, confession or not?"

"I really don't know. All I know is that I have one. I've never had a confession before and this is my—this is...oh, dammit!" The man opened the lid of the recorder and turned it upside down, shaking it. "I forgot the cassette."

"Who *are* you?" Don demanded. "Why were you sniffing around in my closet? And why are you wearing my hat!"

The man bowed. "I am Kirsinov the spy."

Don glanced over at Yoramin. "Another one of you."

"I was raised by government officials to be a spy," Kirsinov continued. "They were my fathers and mothers. I never even knew who my parents were."

"These are the men they pick to be spies," Yoramin said to Don. "Imbeciles."

"Quiet, Yoramin," whispered the priest. "Can't you see that the poor man is crying his eyes out?"

"I never saw my parents," Kirsinov wailed. "The officials never let me do anything. I wanted to go out and play, but they'd say, 'No, go tape somebody.' Bastards! They taught me how to follow people and eavesdrop on people and lie and kill folks. But did they ever love me? No! My life has been such a waste. And if I don't come back with Yoramin, they will take away my eyeballs."

"How gruesome!" the priest exclaimed.

"Oh, no, no. We wear eyeball patches on our upper arm sleeves. See? It is our symbol. Anyway, I must have Yoramin, so let's go. Put your jacket on."

"You'll just have to kill me then," Yoramin said. "Because I'm not coming. I just started living."

"So have I," announced the priest.

"Why don't you start, too? Join us. We're getting the hell out of here."

"They'll send someone else, though," Kirsinov said.

"Let them," Yoramin said.

A smile broke over Kirsinov's face, and he tossed his tape recorder over his shoulder, smashing the priest's bedroom window. Yoramin and the priest rolled their eyes at each other. Outside, Bruce put his ladder down and walked toward the window. "I'll fix it, Father," he called.

An hour later, Don, Yoramin, and Kirsinov were on a bus to the Midwest where they decided to live. They moved every few months at first in order to make it more difficult for future spies to find them. As it was, over the next few years, many spies did find them, but each, like Kirsinov, ended up giving up spying and staying with the group. Many of them married, including Don and Yoramin, and they had many children who played together and went to school together and lived happily. Don opened his own small grocery store. With his mind clear he discovered he could tell jokes for the first time, and he found that once every three or four months he could make a customer chuckle or smirk a little bit. Yoramin became a bus driver and named his first three sons Ivan before his wife complained. As for Ivan Spatulishnotskutchkinitski, he waited patiently for Brezhnev to die and then haunted him. It is an action-packed eternal thriller about one ghost haunting another ghost. But that is another story. The present one is ended.

# HEY, SOUL

If you're anything like me, then maybe you'll be caught off guard when my time comes, and you'll forget to escape my body, thinking, Well, maybe I oughta stay with him and see if he comes around. And by then it could be too late—you trapped within my useless remains, like a dolt. I hope you're smarter than that.

When I was seven, were you floating lazily inside me—because you were only a seven-year-old soul—when I brushed my teeth with Nupercainal? Did you not get why they were laughing when I showed my parents my bright white teeth after brushing with the new "toothpaste?"

Were you paying attention at all, were you ready to flee, when I touched the exposed plug under the couch groping for a ball, and then sat shaking at the kitchen table, eating my pudding and afraid to tell my parents I'd just been jolted?

When the brakes went out on the boss's car, were you ready to time your jump out of me as I raced downhill through the red-lit intersection on Vets Highway, just barely avoiding two cars coming from either side? Or had you been looking at the girls in front of the pizza place while the brakes of other cars screeched? Later, maybe you drifted quietly inside me, ho-hum about it all, while I sat in the car on an uphill grassy slope, my head on the wheel, breathing hard and thanking God my life wasn't over at eighteen. Even if you had been ready, would you have taken me with you, or would you have stuck around with my dead body waiting for the boss's orders—as clueless as I'd been to listen to him about only needing to pump the brakes every once in a while.

Of course you remember fifteen years ago, when my T'ai Chi teacher died, and her oldest student—who'd been at her bedside— told me that he briefly felt her presence in the room when she passed. A few weeks before, he said that she'd exclaimed, "I want to get out of this body." Maybe, I sometimes think, you'd do the same for me.

But she was brilliant, and her soul was certain. You—like me, I suspect—only grope and fumble.

Last week, for instance, I forgot that my car window was closed. I tried to stick my head out like a good driver as I backed out of the driveway, and rammed my forehead against the window, sending my kids into an ice-cream-outing laughing fit. Later, feeling at my sore head and watching the kids slurp their cones, I asked, How could you, my soul, possibly know what to do, where to go, the way my teacher's soul did, if I can't even tell that a window is closed? I imagined myself lying dead and you stumped by walls and ceilings, or lingering like some dumbbell, eternally iffy about that brilliant beckoning light ahead.

I worry about that now sometimes. But I worried most of all ten years ago, during the week I'd been punched out on the Brooklyn Bridge. Rejected by Marion for the eighth or ninth time, forlorn along the pedestrian planks, I hadn't seen that furious bicyclist, built like a truck, barrel toward me, or feel him bounce off me onto the wood slats. Nor did I feel his fists as he came up swinging when I ran over to help him up.

Swollen-eyed and finished with her, but still knowing somehow that she would be my wife, I escaped the city for a week at the fancy upstate hotel and glared at the waiters and waitresses who looked at my black eye and tried not to laugh when they took my order or poured more coffee. I wondered, scowling, if they saw not only the injured eye of an idiot, but his bumbling soul as well. Later, after drinking three or four mudslides, I wondered if you were even with me anymore.

Finally, in the hotel room the next night, after futilely trying to write a postcard to her—a now-or-never postcard, a she's-the-only-girl-for-me postcard—I wondered what would have happened had I not jumped and run clear of the tipping golf cart that I'd driven sideways along a steep hill that morning? Would you have pulled me up with you to climb clear of my crushed body? Or would you have remained useless inside me, a Nothing along with me, having been too preoccupied by the hope that she'd finally say yes to soar out of me in time.

# OUR CARNEGIE HALL CONCERT

I'll tell you what I found most interesting about the Carnegie Hall concert that me and the lady friend just got back from. It was the conductor and how he is the only performer who gets to do a whole show with his back to an audience, except for all the bowing and the walking in and out of backstage doors that he does at the end.

This particular conductor had gray hair, but only the side hair was left and it was fluffy and had plenty of body, like he had used some special show business shampoo and a professional grade blow dryer on it just before the performance. We had a balcony seat, so I was looking right down on top of him, and what kept me from closing my eyes and pretending like I was somewhere else was how whenever the music got a little lively, the conductor began to jump and gyrate around. He waved his arms like an angry traffic cop and snapped his head forward and down like he was trying to give himself a whiplash. Once in a while his feet left the ground and he went airborne like Larry Bird. Meanwhile the two gray side tufts leapt around and up and down like of their own free will.

Whenever the music died down and was beautiful, I settled back in my seat, but when the tension built up and the music went wild again, I sat up straight and opened my eyes wide. In fact, whenever he started the head snapping and the jumping, I wanted to stand all the way up just like they do at baseball games when an exciting play happens. But I saw that no one else was going to do it, so I didn't try.

My lady friend she liked the hair thing too, but her favorite was the violinist, who she wondered didn't break his violin strings because he was pressing down on them so hard. He had a tremendous amount of thick curly hair, so we started to compare his hair to the conductor's, and then we compared their real life hairdos to their hair as portrayed in the programs. It was an interesting two minutes of analysis, but then we got shushed by some fellow ticket holders who said they'd rather hear the music, so we let it go until intermission.

At intermission everyone got up to line up for the bathroom, but we stayed put, mutually deciding to hold it in while we wondered at the people around us and guessed what each one did for a living and what was their names. Some people looked over at us, especially a well-dressed lady with wild eyes and pinched lips, so we guessed that she was an amphetamine tester. We tried not to laugh because she kept staring at us, but it didn't work.

Soon after intermission, when the conductor came out again, I got a little tired of the hair subject as I recalled vaguely that I am losing my own hair, and predicted that now every time I heard that same Brahms violin concerto I would begin to fret about my own shedding rooftop.

Before I knew it and maybe because I was sleeping, the concerto ended with a long loud note. I was up and around in time to see the conductor begin his practice of going out through a door after all the clapping starts, and then coming back in like he forgot something and is surprised when everyone starts clapping all over again. Next he went out the door with the violinist, and the violinist came back in again like *he* forgot something. And then the conductor came in after him and that really got the crowd going. My lady

184

friend she liked the conductor going in and out like that too, but her favorite was how the violinist bowed: he took so long to decide to bow and then just eased his head down very slowly like he was afraid to break his neck, unlike the conductor who seemed to have no fear for his spinal column.

The clapping went on for a long time, and it was getting late, so we squeezed past our row of standing ovation givers and headed for the exit while all the bowing and the walking in and out of doors was still going on.

I told my lady friend that all in all I thought it was a pretty nice concert and she agreed, but we also agreed that we'd forgotten how all the melodies went. My lady friend she said so what's the point if you can't remember any of the songs, and I had to say that I agreed with her.

# SUBURBAN AMERICA (A NOVEL)

## Book I

A disenchanted would-be poet and his Great Dane move in. Neighbors wave hello from their yards. Several laminated "No Trespassing" signs appear on quarter-acre lawns. A radio control plane tournament goes bad. Sour-faced town constable stops by.

Two bumbling librarians often knock heads reaching for the same book. Someone's lazy beer-drinking stepfather flips out of a hammock. A friendly old woman with a bum knee lives quietly with her disinterested cat. An unpopular wedding is the talk of the block. A drunken scene at the reception results. The overturned table gets the brunt of it. Multiple apologies turn into fresh arguments. Three rainy chapters in a row.

## Book II

The theft of a lawnmower. Office elevator out of order. Sarcastic repairman arrives. Man saves woman from crazed poodle. A romance that will never work out. Not enough sun for the garden. Three hours late to a funeral. Nightmare in a dentist's chair. A rich uncle with a temper. Multiple restraining orders served to several characters for several distances. Cell phones that just won't work. A fly too fast to swat with a towel. Kid insists his dog can talk.

## Book III

Too much advice from a best friend. A con man with red hair and a sardonic grin, just passing through. Torn "No Trespassing" signs. Angry constable. A kind-hearted blond-haired cop that we immediately like. Very smart child who irritates adults. Deli workers compete to serve salami to the same pretty woman. A shouting match over a weather forecast. Three chapters of text messages.

Four runaway Chihuahuas. A rabbit that keeps getting into only one character's garden. Super-laminated "No Trespassing" signs are reinstalled. A mailbox is stuffed with crud. The arrest of an innocent man. Beleaguered town constable. Elevators still out of order. Sarcastic repairman out to lunch.

## Book IV

Still no hope for the romance. A drunken rant at a party. Straight jacket not necessary. Malevolent horse fly wreaks havoc at the pool. An out-of-control lawnmower causes a mad scramble. Somebody's cousin allergic to bromine; another's cousin allergic to lava. Poet's new girlfriend makes ginger cookies for neighbors. Three freshly cemented "Private Property" signs appear side by side. Con man gets conned by very smart kid. Blond-haired cop knew it all along. Poet moves to the big city. Homemade cookies tossed en masse. Slick new neighbor with a Harley moves into poet's old house. His tulips are torn to pieces at 4 a.m. Purple-faced constable resigns. Philosophical characters rap in a laundromat. Meryl Streep and Kevin Bacon make cameos. Someone's lawn has turned brown. High school kid's grandmother makes a complete fool of herself at his graduation. Romance might work out after all. Elevator still won't work. Two characters decide to take the stairs.

# CRAVING HONEY

During my brief Yoga era, it was my Thursday evening habit to roam the hallways of the famous C___ Hall during the fifteen minutes or so before seven o'clock class and sit on the third step of the black-and-white marble staircase. I'd take my coffee and donut out of the already coffee-soaked brown bag, peal the sports section from under my arm, and chew and sip and read.

But on one of these Thursdays, the acting class behind the closed door in front of me caught my attention. Male voices and female voices went through exercises, during which they repeated—softly or full-lunged, earnestly or with disgust—the same phrases or the same questions and answers. At first I thought it was all real and sat up, alarmed.

"I hate you," a man's voice said matter-of-factly.

"I hate you," another said in the same tone.

"Get out of my house!" the first man screamed, and I looked around, my eyebrows knit.

"Get out of my house!" the other echoed, adding extra umph to the "out."

Then, softly..."You make me sad."

"You make me sad..."

"You make me so sad," the first said again, this time with melo-dramatic syrup.

"You make me oh-so sad," the other repeated, on the verge of boo-hooing.

It wasn't until I heard laughter behind the door when I realized that, after all, I was in C___ Hall, and music and acting and dancing and Yoga were everywhere, so I relaxed.

I returned each week with my coffee and donut and newspaper and flipped through the sports section, listening with pleasure to the screaming and the crying within. When there was particular anguish or harshness, I looked up from my paper.

"You have absolutely *crippled* me!" an actress cried shrilly from within on the third or fourth week. Then she said it again, without prompting, in a different, weepy tone, and then said it a third time, incredulously.

"Make up your mind, lady, how you feel about being crippled," I muttered, my voice echoing up the stairway.

Yoga classes had begun to bore me because I couldn't direct my foot anywhere near my head from any angle, so on Thursday eve-nings it became of secondary interest to that pleasurable before-time on the stairway when I listened to them—different actors' voices, almost each time—cajole and berate and tease and complain and holler and accuse. Art in the making, I nodded knowingly.

When the shrill, crippled actress returned after a brief two-week hiatus from her misery, her voice had lowered an octave. She spoke softly.

"The beach is nice," she said.

"The beach is nice," a male voice repeated, but with a harsh rasp.

"The beach is nice," she said again, her voice even softer, and I felt my blood pressure taking a much-needed dive.

"It's very nice," he rasped at her, and I thought, Shut up and let her talk.

192

"It's very nice," her voice said, with extra honey, and I was in love.

There were worse things than being in love with the shrill, silky voice of a crippled actress. I comforted myself like that when I returned the following week, this time at six-thirty, with a hamburger, coffee, and a raspberry tart. I forgot to bring the newspaper.

This time, however, instead of hearing her shrill or honey voice, I heard two men's voices, and I became a sourpuss, rolling my eyes and munching my hamburger while a Richard Burton type and a Peter O'Toole type went back and forth about dumplings or something. I was only half-listening.

"I didn't order the damn dumplings!" Richard Burton may have shouted.

"Then what are they doing here?" roared Peter O'Toole.

I shrugged, reasoning that these two seasoned actors had dropped their repeat-after-me routine and had advanced into full-fledged scripts.

"How the hell should I know?" Richard Burton said sharply.

"Where's Karen?"

"How dare you—"

"What did you do with her?" cried O'Toole.

I sat up, chewing and chewing my hamburger. It was like old radio, and I hoped that the sweet, shrill, crippled actress in question was Karen, and that she'd chime in at any moment and talk about the beach.

But instead one of them mumbled something I didn't quite get. It was either, "Go blow your nose," or "So the crow knows."

There was a gunshot sound—and my heart jumped—followed many seconds later by a faint thud, then silence. Just as I was figuring that they were about to try that part over again, the door flew open and a man, either Burton or O'Toole, burst out and pulled the door closed after him. His face was set hard and he glanced up at me briefly. I lip-smiled, raising my eyebrows and nodding my appreciation, and then listened to him race down the stairs behind me on the other side of the hall.

I looked at my watch. Ten minutes to seven. There was no beach-loving Karen-voice, no sound at all from the room. The show was over for the week, it seemed, so I headed over to my stupid Yoga class.

I have a sort of sixth sense about things, so it was no surprise to me when I returned to the stairway the next few weeks with only a coffee, and spent two or three silent minutes in front of that plain black door. No voices came from within, so I moped my way through each Yoga class. Jeanne the instructor, an older woman who nonetheless could reach her big toe to her ear without a squawk, wondered aloud what on earth was wrong with me. Why was I so blue, she wanted to know, and why couldn't I twist myself to look like a caduceus? I just shrugged.

One evening after class, I squeezed into the elevator crowded with artists from the floors above, and just before we reached the bottom, a woman's voice behind taller heads said to someone, "Saturday is beach weather." I almost snapped my neck looking for her through the thick crowd, and I lost her among the five or six women who got off the elevator and scattered along Seventh Avenue.

I walked home all fifty-seven blocks downtown, thinking of that voice, still in existence after all, practicing her voice-art on a higher floor. I counted out the possible number of studios multiplied by the number of floors above the Yoga floor, but was snapped out of my calculations by some drunk guy sitting against a wall near 14th Street and Third Avenue.

"Hey man," he said as I passed. "If my head was shaped like yours, I'd wear a hat."

The next week I was all business, arriving at six o'clock and starting from the seventh floor, listening carefully outside each black studio door. I had a newspaper with me, so when anyone abruptly came out of a studio or walked down the hallway, I held up the sports section and cursed the Mets under my breath.

By the time I reached the twelfth floor, my legs were tired from the climbing, my mouth was tired from muttering about the Mets, and my insides ached. I'd already forgotten what she'd sounded like, and my class had already begun, so I sat dourly on the stairs, imagining Jeanne urging me to cheer up. I blew a raspberry at her just as a group of men and women appeared at a studio to my left. They looked over at me curiously before going inside. "Bunch of busybodies," I grumped after the door slammed.

I leaned back, my elbows against a step, and decided to philosophize instead of going to Yoga. Everyone had their own talents, I mused, their own art, and the art of speaking with a silky voice was unlike any other art. A listener who tries to re-experience the deep pang into the stomach a beautiful voice once gave him will fail every time. On the plus side, a horrid voice that can send chills through a person can only be felt in the moment too. The chills don't return, only the memory of the words themselves, of the tone itself. I remembered but couldn't re-experience how I'd felt during my teen years when I passed a pretty girl on a Long Island street. She'd seemed so easy-going and gentle, and I lifted my chin, about to say hello as I passed, but her face twisted up and her head sprang from side to side. "Watta you lookin' at!"

Voices came from behind the door to my left. The people I had raspberried laughed a little, and then a male voice droned on for a while, stopping the laughter cold. I sat up and unfolded my newspaper, not reading. There was silence for a while before the droning male voice said casually, "Are you eating my omelet?"

"Are you eating my omelet?" a second male voice repeated, in a colder tone.

"Eat my omelet," the first urged gently, and I knit my brows.

"Eat the damn omelet!" the second voice roared, and I curled my lip at the force of his tone and growled, "That's right, you bum, eat that omelet."

There was a pause. Then another, familiar voice softly chimed in. "I like scrambled," she said, and that pang, her pang, went through me again. I sighed and waited, trying to guess which of the women she'd been among the group receiving my raspberry. "I do so like scrambled," she went on.

"I like poached," the first male voice complained, pouting.

"I like scrambled...eggs...very much," she purred, and my mouth fell open.

"You know," broke in the second male voice with rising rage, "I'd like to smear these eggs all over your stupid *face*!" I sat upright.

"You know..." she crooned, and I slumped back pudding-like against the stairs. "I'd like to smear these eggs all over your...extremely...stupid...face." I pressed my palm over one eye.

I had found her again, and so I went back the next week, passing the Yoga floor without a thought and heading to the same twelfth-floor stairway. There were already voices coming from inside the studio when I arrived.

"All right, punk," said a voice, almost exactly like Clint East-wood's. "There was a banana muffin on that table. I'll give you two seconds—"

"I don't know where your damn muffin is," another voice cut in. He sounded a little like Buddy Hackett.

"Maybe your girlfriend ate it," said Eastwood, and I grumbled to myself, "Now it's muffins."

"You should mind your own—*stinking* business about Karen," cried Hackett.

"What did you say?"

"Mind your own stinking—"

"That's what I thought you said."

196

There were prolonged gasping, gagging, and strangulated kinds of noises from behind the door, and I sat there on the stairs rolling my eyes, waiting for Buddy Hackett to die. Finally, there was a heavy thud, and silence for a while. I tilted my head from side to side impatiently, waiting. And then the door flew open and a man, the same guy who'd killed Peter O'Toole or Richard Burton, walked out and shut the door quickly behind. He glowered up at me for a second as he went by and then raced down the stairs, and I kind of smirked after him.

During my long walk home, I decided that it wasn't worth hanging around weeks between murders for Karen to chime in just once and make my insides go all gooey. Her voice was rare art, yes, but maybe not worth waiting through the same old scripts to get to one soft-toned, honey coo. I was fully into this train of thought, sorry for myself and enjoying my yearning—complete with strings and woodwinds—for so much more from life than the ordinary, when I passed the corner of 14th Street and Third Avenue, and that same drunk, sitting against the wall, startled me as I went by.

"Hey man," he said, and I rolled my eyes. "If my head was shaped like yours...I'd wear a bag over it."

# TONY THE MUSTACHE

Tony didn't have a mustache. Tony was the mustache, so I hope you don't think the title of this story needs correction. Tony was a thick, bristly, sparkling black mustache, and he was connected to the upper lip of a man named Anthony. Anthony was always called Anthony by his friends and others, so Tony chose the name for himself—first to establish his own identity and individuality; at the same time Tony didn't want to insult his master, even though Anthony had no idea that Tony had given himself a name. Tony simply would have felt guilty not to identify with his master in some way. After all, if it weren't for Anthony, Tony could just as well have been a bunch of small black bristles clinging to the sides of the sink every morning, only to have Anthony's wife smother them with her hand and scream, "Will you wash out the goddamn sink after you finish shaving, Anthony!" And her voice would fade to nothing as parts of Tony slid down the drain.

Tony shivered at the thought of being shaved, and each time he shivered, Anthony would touch him, sometimes scratch him, up and down, up and down. "Stupid mustache itches like hell," he'd say, and scratch and scratch as Tony, in agony, would writhe and shift, and Anthony would scratch even more. And when it was all over, Tony would sit quietly, exhausted, not daring to make another move.

Tony lived in constant apprehension. As a result, he was a very jumpy mustache. He had horrible nightmares a few times a week, sometimes more. One nightmare in particular was a recurring one. While Anthony was shaving the rest of his face, the razor grinned at Tony between the double blades, repeating, "Whoops, slipped, got the mustache. Whoops." And then the razor laughed fiendishly. Tony awoke from such nightmares in excruciating pain while Anthony, half-asleep, scratched at him.

Tony could be described as a nervous wreck of a mustache, though his master would often only refer to him as "this stupid mustache," which sometimes left Tony depressed for days on end.

The other mustaches Tony encountered all seemed to be more at ease. He'd pass them on the street as Anthony strolled to and from his office and the subway. "How ya doin'," many of the mustaches would ask as they passed one another. Tony wondered why most of them were so cheerful. Some were very religious, he knew. One mustache on a shopping line had tried to tell Tony about the Lord, that He saved mustaches as well as sinners.

"What about sinful mustaches?" Tony asked sardonically. The other mustache, flustered, told Tony to suit himself, then—that he'd go to hell and be scratched for eternity. Tony told him to get lost. Stupid blond mustaches, he thought, but he half-believed what it had told him about an eternal scratching.

Other mustaches he knew were just plain idiotic. They seemed so satisfied just sitting there on their masters' upper lips, not even realizing that they were helpless, that they were at the mercy of their masters' whims and couldn't even go to a baseball game if they wanted to, that they would be shaved out of existence someday, maybe even before breakfast, and that it could happen at any time, without reason.

One mustache in particular caused Tony to convulse into a fit of anger. It happened inside an elevator in the building where Anthony worked. Two other mustaches were there. One of the mustaches said to the other, "My master's going to shave me off later."

"Really?" the second mustache said.

"His girlfriend's been on his case about shaving me off, so he agreed."

"Oh well," said the second.

"We all have to go sometime," the first said, and both mustaches chuckled.

Tony was fuming. "Don't you care at all, you idiots? You just accept it, just like that?"

"What do you want me to do?" the first mustache said. "I can't do anything about it. We all have to get shaved off sometime, so you might as well accept it, or else you'll turn gray earlier than you think."

"Who cares?" Tony said.

The two mustaches got off the elevator with their masters as another mustache got on. It was Ray, Tony's best friend. Anthony talked with Ray's master Clay every day. "You look a little down in the bristles, Tone," Ray said.

"I am."

"Thinking about being shaved again?"

"What else?"

"Look, I told you. Stop reading that Sartre."

"I can't help it. Anthony's reading *Being and Nothingness*."

"You don't have to read it. Curl your hairs."

They both stopped their conversation when overhearing Ray's master Clay say to Anthony. "Hey, your mustache is all tangled up in knots, man. You're really letting it go. Why don't you trim it up, make it look nice? Look at my mustache. It's all combed out and shampooed. Yours looks like the cat dragged it in."

"I don't know. It's getting to be a pain. It was a good idea to start with but...I don't know. I think I'm going to get rid of it—just close my eyes and shave it off. Zip-zip-zip, and be done with it."

Tony gasped and shivered and Anthony scratched him.

"See?" Anthony said. "It's itchy as hell. Michelle says I look like Hitler with it."

"Hitler?" Clay said.

"Yeah. It's definitely got to go soon."

"Ray!" Tony exclaimed. "It's over! It's over!"

"Take it easy, pal," Ray said.

"Damn, and I'm getting a cold, too," Anthony said as he sniffed twice and let out a hard sneeze. The elevator had stopped, and Anthony and Clay got out. Mucus had spurted out of Anthony's nose all over Tony. As Clay and Anthony parted, Tony looked helplessly at Ray through the curtain, like a veil of death, which had fallen from the very roof under which Tony lived. The very stuffings of Anthony's nose had coated Tony with the seal of his fate. And though Anthony wiped the mucus off with his sleeve, Tony still felt sticky with it. The smell of mucus and death was in the air, and Tony settled into a profound despair which lasted the rest of the day.

That night when Anthony kissed his wife hello, she said, "Oh, Anthony, that mustache itches like hell. I hate it more every day."

"You're not so hot yourself, toots," Tony said, although of course she couldn't hear him.

"You look just like Hitler," she said.

"Hitler? Then I'd better shave it."

"Good."

Stupid woman, Tony thought. If it weren't for you he wouldn't shave me off. It's your fault, all your fault. Hitler's mustache was a dwarf anyway. I'm no dwarf. How blind can you be?

"I'll shave it in the morning," Anthony sighed.

Tony didn't sleep all that night. He philosophized, brooded, even settled into a sort of calm resignation as the approach of his death neared.

Mustaches are sort of helpless, Tony thought. There's nothing we can do about our existence. We start as nubs, unaware of ourselves, though the experts say our personalities are shaped during the nub period. Then we grow into awkward, confused, separate bristles, not knowing what to do with all our stiff, stubby hairs. Later we mature—we get our hairs together, unifying into a whole, fully-grown mustache. We are given life, and we either live it to the fullest, day by day, throughout all the anguish and the pain, growing old and gray and, if we are lucky, dying with our masters, or else we die early, always much too young. And it's always at the hands of those guys who just want to see how we look on them, and who murder us soon after, the butchers. We are completely helpless, unable to control the ways of fate.

But, thought Tony, I've learned only now that, though helpless, a mustache can enjoy his life to the fullest. I think back and wonder why I didn't enjoy that last shower more, and why so many times I slept, saying, "The hell with this," while Anthony was making love to his wife, when I could have hung around and observed or laughed at the stupid things they said. And why didn't I enjoy all that spaghetti sauce that always splashed on me whenever Anthony ate spaghetti? Why? Because I was too self-centered, too narcissistic a mustache to enjoy any of those things. Oh, if only a mustache could write a book, could tell the story of a mustache as told *by* a mustache, then the world would see. But now all that is lost.

The day broke, and by this time Tony was fully prepared and calm. Anthony rose, walked to the bathroom, and contemplated his reflection in the mirror. Tony tried to be brave, as brave as any mustache could be. Anthony grabbed his razor and began to wet Tony, and Tony closed his eyes.

POOR ADVICE AND OTHER STORIES

Silence. Then, "I can't do it," Anthony said. "For some crazy reason I like this stupid mustache. I'll keep it." He shaved the rest of his face and then put the razor away.

Tony could not contain himself. He beamed. He kicked up his follicles. "Whoopee! Yahoo!"

As Anthony came out of the subway and walked down the street, Tony screamed, "Yippee! I'm alive! I'm alive! However painful it all is, however miserable and helpless we all are, we are still alive!"

One mustache looked at Tony and cursed him out, and Tony saw a reflection of his former self in that mustache. He'll learn, he thought, if he doesn't get shaved off first.

When Anthony entered the office building, Tony heard Ray's high-pitched scream. Across the lobby Clay drank, soaking Ray with boiling hot coffee. Tony laughed and called out, "Ray! Ray!" not able to wait to give his friend the news.

# THIS IS MY MONTAUK

Jackie's sixth floor apartment on Chrystie Street was dusty, moldy, chain-smoke-filled, cat-hairy and cat-urine-y; and Jackie herself hacked and hawked between sentences, sitting on her bed and telling Jim, who'd known her dead son, and Glen, Jim's friend, all about that bastard landlord's refusal to paint the apartment unless she got rid of her two cats. Glen stood close to the door, trying to breathe only shallowly against the smoke, hoping the visit would be a short one, and that he and Jim would be on their way downstairs and across the park to watch the Chrystie Street basketball tournament. But Jim's friend, Jackie's son, had died of an overdose only a few months before, and this was his friend's mother. Jim looked at Glen, who already knew what Jim was going to say.

"Let's go get some paint."

It wasn't only paint that they later hauled upstairs after two trips to a Canal Street hardware store: it was the paint scraper and the primer and several brushes and turpentine and a tarp.

"Eddie was a good friend of mine," Jim explained, stopping Glen from paying for paint on the second trip.

"All right," Glen said. "I'm there."

Glen was there, helping Jim set up and move the furniture away from the walls, but when he tried to open the two windows for some air, neither one would budge. Jackie offered them Pepsi in cloudy glasses, and Glen set his down on a table. Jackie sat on her bed, smoking a cigarette down to the end, then immediately light-ing another. Glen tried not to breathe much, wondering how long the job would take, and how much smoke and fumes and toxins and disease was going to seep into his body during this afternoon of painting.

"Where're the ladders, boys?" Jackie laughed, and her laughter turned into a red-faced coughing fit. Jim and Glen looked at each other, chuckled, and headed for the door, Glen himself coughing out the smoke on his way out.

Two ladders-borrowed-from-the-Super later, Glen stood on the last step of one to paint near the ceiling. He'd tried chipping away old paint first, but a large chunk of plaster came down with one scrape, so he painted over everything, cracks, bumps, and all. He looked behind, relieved to see Jim painting without bothering to scrape either. Maybe it would only be a two hour job.

It was hot and stuffy, though, and every time Jackie hacked, Glen held his breath against the germs.

"She's sick," Jim had told him on the way up the stairs with the ladders. "Real sick."

"Oh," was all Glen said, tight-jawed, imagining himself coughing uncontrollably one day, and recalling what started it—the marathon paint job on Chrystie Street.

He grew quieter while painting, only half-smiling at the stories Jackie told from the bed and laughing a little through his nose at her punch lines. Sweat poured down his face, but he let the Pepsi rest in the glass on the coffee table, dust and paint and cat hair and disease inside it already, he thought. He painted faster, slapping it on, while Jackie, not seeming to care how haphazardly he painted, talked on and on.

Later Jim and Jackie were talking baseball, and Glen looked over. It was all about the World Series, starting that night, and Jackie bragged that she'd never been wrong. The Reds would win it this year, she said firmly. She was sure that her favorite, Lou Piniella, would have her boys ready to win.

Glen laughed, coming down the ladder a step. "Not a chance," he said, turning back for a final stroke of paint before stepping down all the way to move the ladder.

"Not only win," Jackie said, and coughed loosely. "But *sweep.*"

"Oh, jeez, not a chance," Glen said. "The A's will sweep if *either* team will."

"Wanna make a wager on that?" Jackie smiled.

"What?"

"Wanna bet?"

"No. Bet what?" He stopped painting.

Jackie coughed for a while before answering. "Case of cigarettes."

"The Reds won't win."

"One case of cigarettes."

"All right." Glen shrugged.

"And if you win, I'll cook you a nice meal."

"Oh...all right." Glen stared for a moment at her smiling face, then turned back to hook up the roller to paint the wall. He looked at the impossible-to-open windows.

"Reds have no chance, though," he warned her between shallow breaths.

"We'll see," she said after taking a deep wheezing one.

It was almost dark when Glen and Jim sat on a bench in Chrystie Street Park with coffee and bread from the Grand Street bakery. Glen's back and arms ached, and he laughed at a twinge that caught him between the shoulder blades when he sat up.

"What's funny?" Jim asked, looking at the basketball courts where stray games were played, the tournament having ended hours before.

"My back's funny," Glen said, glancing at a group huddled near a railing—an exchange between quick hands. "Lot of drugs here," he said under his breath.

Jim nodded. "Lot of everything here, though. You only see one thing sometimes." He looked around. "Eddie was a good guy. And she's a good lady."

Glen shifted on the bench and leaned his elbows on his knees. He nodded slowly. "Yeah, she's nice," he said at last. "And it was good exercise...except for all the smoke."

"It's tough. Parents...they're not supposed to bury their kids."

Glen frowned, glancing over again at the huddled group which had now broken apart, going their separate ways. He sat back again, sipping.

"Coffee's pretty good. Maybe we'll get a couple of more."

Jim nodded, looking out at the park and then past it. "This is my Montauk," he said.

Glen was quiet, and he looked around with Jim at the handball courts and at the many basketball rims without nets. He looked at the old men sitting on green paint-chipped benches, and at the paper-and-leaf-strewn stone pavement, and at the lane of trees that lined the path parallel to Chrystie Street. "This is my Montauk," Jim repeated, looking all around. "They can all have their beach vacations, their Hamptons and their Bermudas and their Bahamas and whatever else. This is my Montauk...right here. I'll take it."

Glen took a deep breath and let it out very slowly between slightly parted lips. Looking past two dealers walking toward the other side of the park, he realized that the darkness had already settled in.

The Reds won the World Series four games to none, and when Glen stopped to talk with Jim in the street a month later, Jim reminded him about the bet.

"But isn't she sick?" Glen said. "How about a case of orange juice instead? Or soup."

"A bet's a bet, man," Jim said. "She wants her cigarettes."

"Right."

But another month went by and Glen forgot all about the cigarettes, and another went by and Jim and Glen went for a coffee on a not-so-cold January Saturday. Again they sat in the park, and after an hour Jim mentioned that Jackie had died.

"Oh," Glen said, and was quiet for a while. "Crap."

"She wanted to go," Jim said casually, looking past Glen at the trees. "Her son was gone."

"That stinks."

"She didn't want to be here."

"I never paid her the cigarettes."

Jim shrugged.

"I thought they were bad for her, so..."

Jim looked over at Glen with a knowing smile. "She was on her way out," he said. "She wanted her cigarettes."

Glen frowned out into the park.

"Can't stop it when it's your time," Jim went on matter-of-factly from somewhere behind Glen's slowly shaking head.

Glen stood in the center of the subway platform, staring blindly at the crowd and waiting for the Chrystie Street train back home to Brooklyn. His focus fell on the yellow-painted line that ran along the end of the platform, and then he noticed the many people who had stepped across it. Some of them leaned their bodies out over the edge, looking for signs of the downtown train. Glen shuddered, planting his feet firmly in the center of the platform.

*All it would take, you idiots, is one maniac to walk by and give you a little shove. One slipup, just one off-balance-making poke with a forefinger and that would be it, you fools.*

The train heading uptown roared in, and Glen sneered at the clustered groups that craned their necks or stretched whole torsos over the edge for a glimpse of the downtown.

"It's coming anyway," he spat out to them, barely hearing himself amidst the roar. "It'll come whether you look or not."

# ACKNOWLEDGEMENTS

I would like to thank the editors of the following literary magazines where the stories in this collection first appeared.

*Waccamaw Journal*: "Hands"
*Eclectica Magazine*: "The Lady with the Red Van"
*Prick of the Spindle*: "A Lost Flokati"
*Stirring: A Literary Collection*: "Poor Advice"
*Blue Lake Review*: "Letters from a Young Poet"
*The Cortland Review*: "Squeezing the Boots"
*Loch Raven Review*: "Days of Wine and Pratfalls"
*Untoward Magazine*: "Correspondence" and "A Teen Tale"
*Hawai'i Review*: "Never Trust a Pool Salesman"
*Umbrella Factory Magazine, 2011*: "Little Leagues"
*Cobalt Review, 2014*: "Little Leagues"
*Rose & Thorn Journal*: "Orca (A Madcap Thriller)"
*Sand Canyon Review*: "The Wrong Beth"
*Forge Journal*: "Wannabes"
*Foliate Oak Magazine*: "Our Carnegie Hall Concert"
*Breakwater Review*: "The Flip Side"
*Halfway Down the Stairs*: "Making Change"
*Two Hawks Quarterly*: "Hey, Soul"
*Spilling Ink Review*: "The Fly Massacre"
*Rougarou*: "The Spy and the Priest"
*The Bicycle Review*: "Tony the Mustache"
*The Legendary*: "Suburban America (A Novel)"
*Bartleby Snopes*: "The Ventriloquist,"
"With Doleful Vexation" and "Craving Honey"

# A READER'S GUIDE TO POOR ADVICE

1.  How does the narrator's description of the opera in "Poor Advice" reveal his feelings about his present life?

2.  Who are the antagonists in "Making Change," "Letters from a Young Poet," "The Spy and the Priest," and "Orca." Explain how each is an antagonist.

3.  Choose two stories in the collection that have a common theme. Identify and explain how each story fits the theme.

4.  Does the protagonist in "Letters from a Young Poet" undergo a change? Is he the same person on his return trip that he was when he arrived in Italy? Defend your answer with evidence from the story.

5.  Choose from among "The Flip Side," "Orca," and "The Wrong Beth." Identify a character who acts as a foil, and explain what strength or weakness in the main character he or she reveals.

6.  Choose two stories from the collection and identify one internal and one external conflict in each.

7.  Identify the flashbacks used in "Little Leagues" and "Squeezing the Boots." How do the flashbacks in each story help reveal more about the narrators?

8.  Where might an epiphany occur in "The Flip Side" or "Letters from a Young Poet?" Explain your answer.

9.  How does the mood of "Making Change" contrast with the mood of "This Is My Montauk?" Explain your answer using evidence from both stories.

10. How may "The Spy and the Priest," "Tony the Mustache," and "Suburban America" be considered satires?

11. Identify a story in the collection that contains an unreliable narrator? In what way is this narrator unreliable?

12. A character may fantasize about a situation while doing something ordinary. The narrator in "Making Change," for example, sits on a park bench fantasizing about a conversation between two characters who were hostile to him. Write an "ordinary" scene during which a character slips into a fantasy that is related to how he or she feels.

13. Identify some of the flat characters that appear in "Squeezing in the Boots," "The Flip Side," "A Lost Flokati, and "Hands." What are their roles in each story?

14. Outline or diagram the plot of "With Doleful Vexation," "The Ventriloquist," or "The Spy and the Priest." Identify the conflict, the rising action, the climax, and the resolution.

15. Choose one of the quotes (by Ring Lardner or Aldous Huxley) that appears in the front section of the book. Apply its meaning to two of the stories in the collection.

# PRAISE FOR POOR ADVICE

Shake yourself free from the restraints of the ordinary—enter the clever and oh-so-quirky mind of Lou Gaglia and his oddly-so, strangely-so, poignant cast of characters.

— Kathryn Magendie, author of Sweetie

The downtrodden characters that populate Poor Advice chisel away at their blue-collar circumstances and by stories end, without your consent, there's a fissure splintering your heart. Lou Gaglia's a spellbinding writer who gathers material from the underbelly gutter-stuff and conjures up a bit of hope for the hopeless, a place to call home from the homeless, and a fighter's chance at love for the lonely strangers who are, after all, a lot like us.

— Jason Ockert, author of Wasp Box

What I like best about the people and places that populate Lou Gaglia's Poor Advice is that they're all familiar to me. But this is no mean familiarity. Anything but, in fact. These are the people that you meet in your dreams and the places you've visited only in your imagination: people who fail to see the big picture, obsess over one random-seeming detail of their daily routine, are occasionally an orca. It's nice to get to know them better.

— Matt Rowan, author of Big Venerable

Lou Gaglia has a knack for taking mundane, everyday tasks—
like pumping gas, selling pools, and getting your car repaired—and
turning them into the funniest and most damn profound stories
you've ever read. Don't let the title fool you. Gaglia's stories are full
of good advice. Just don't take any of them too seriously or you may
find your life in shambles.

—Nathaniel Tower, author of Nagging Wives, Foolish Husbands

In Poor Advice and Other Stories, Lou Gaglia puts the enter-
tainment back in literary fiction. Many of his characters seem
laughable and misguided in their fumbling ways, especially with
regard to their attempts at approaching the opposite sex, but the
reader will come to love them for their heart-warming innocence.
You will laugh, you will cry, but mostly you will go away remembering his vivid characters, his spot on dialogue, and his varying
modes of conveying the stories in this unique collection, all of
which reflect the talents of an outstanding fiction writer.

— Mitchell Waldman, author of Petty Offenses & Crimes of the
Heart

His readers will find in Lou Gaglia's Poor Advice a new voice in
contemporary short fiction, a voice made memorable by its sensitivity to language as it is spoken today, yet expressing the old veri-
ties of the human heart.

— Earl Ingersoll, Emeritus Distinguished Professor of English,
State University of New York at Brockport.

Made in the USA
Lexington, KY
14 June 2016